Get Your
Coventry Romances
Home Subscription NOW

And Get These
4 Best-Selling Novels
FREE:

LACEY
by Claudette Williams

THE ROMANTIC WIDOW
by Mollie Chappell

HELENE
by Leonora Blythe

THE HEARTBREAK TRIANGLE
by Nora Hampton

A Home Subscription! It's the easiest and most convenient way to get every one of the exciting Coventry Romance Novels! ...And you get 4 of them FREE!

You pay nothing extra for this convenience: there are no additional charges...you don't even pay for postage! Fill out and send us the handy coupon now, and we'll send you 4 exciting Coventry Romance novels absolutely FREE!

SEND NO MONEY, GET THESE
FOUR BOOKS FREE!

- -

C1280

MAIL THIS COUPON TODAY TO:
COVENTRY HOME SUBSCRIPTION SERVICE 6 COMMERCIAL STREET HICKSVILLE, NEW YORK 11801

YES, please start a Coventry Romance Home Subscription in my name. and send me FREE and without obligation to buy, my 4 Coventry Romances. If you do not hear from me after I have examined my 4 FREE books. please send me the 6 new Coventry Romances each month as soon as they come off the presses. I understand that I will be billed only $10.50 for all 6 books. There are no shipping and handling nor any other hidden charges. There is no minimum number of monthly purchases that I have to make. In fact. I can cancel my subscription at any time. The first 4 FREE books are mine to keep as a gift. even if I do not buy any additional books.

For added convenience. your monthly subscription may be charged automatically to your credit card.

☐ Master Charge   ☐ Visa

Credit Card #_____

Expiration Date_____

Name_____
(Please Print)

Address_____

City_____State_____Zip_____

Signature_____

☐ Bill Me Direct Each Month

This offer expires March 31, 1981. Prices subject to change without notice. Publisher reserves the right to substitute alternate FREE books. Sales tax collected where required by law. Offer valid for new members only.

DANGEROUS LADY

Barbara Hazard

FAWCETT COVENTRY • NEW YORK

DANGEROUS LADY

Published by Fawcett Coventry Books, a unit of CBS Publications, the Consumer Publishing Division of CBS Inc.

Copyright © 1980 by Barbara Hazard

All Rights Reserved

ISBN: 0-449-50120-5

Printed in the United States of America

First Fawcett Coventry printing: December 1980

10 9 8 7 6 5 4 3 2 1

FOR DON

with thanks for his understanding,
encouragement, and love.

CHAPTER 1

Problems at Wardley Hall

The fire snapped suddenly, and a log shifted in the grate; the only sound in the library, although there were several people assembled in the room. As if the falling log released some frozen pantomine, the faded lady seated in the wing chair near the fire raised her damp handkerchief to her eyes and sniffed audibly. She was dressed in deep mourning which could not be said to be complimentary. The black gown seemed to call attention to her thin, lined face and the graying hair which she wore severely banded under a sober cap. Across from her, a younger lady sat poised on the edge of her chair, and near her a boy and a little girl stood close together, looking frightened and bewildered. Everyone's attention was riveted on a thin, elderly gentleman, sedately dressed in gray, who was busily straightening some papers on the desk before him, his eyes lowered as if he had no desire to continue the discussion that had been taking place. The silence remained unbroken except for the older lady's soft sobbing for a moment longer, and then the young woman threw out her hands in an impatient gesture and rose, asking in an incredulous tone, "Is it true? There is no money?"

The elderly lawyer, for so he was, coughed deprecatingly and looked at her reluctantly. "As I have explained to you, Miss Ward, there is a little money. A very little!" he added, as if she might mistake the matter and rush into an orgy of spending. Glancing around the library, he could see that a great deal of money would have to be spent if Wardley Hall was ever to return to its former magnificence. The rug had visible holes, the chintz of the draperies and slipcovers was so faded as to make determining the original patterns an impossibility, and the last time the room had been painted must have surely been before her father came into his inheritance.

"But . . . but we always thought . . . I mean, Papa said . . ." she stopped in confusion as the lawyer, Mr. Bentley, gave her a sorrowing glance. He had no intention of spelling out to a young and innocent daughter where the money had gone over the years. Robert Ward had been brought up in luxury, and no amount of lecturing and reproof could bring him to accept that the funds he had always drawn on were fast becoming depleted by an expensive wife, bad investments, indifferent estate agents, gambling and all the other amusements he felt were his due. Mr. Bentley had often wished he were not tied to such an improvident client, even as he was swayed by his charm, for Robert Ward would laugh at all his strictures and gaily say that his latest scheme would pull them all from the River Tick in grand style, and Bentley was not to worry his head about it, but merely loan him a trifling sum for a few weeks, and then he would see! He had been a handsome man with a winning smile, a high color, and a head of black curls which all his children had inherited. His wife Anne had been the toast of London in her first season; a lovely blonde without a serious thought in her head to worry her. Bentley remembered how he had stressed the importance of marrying an heiress, and how Robert Ward had laughed at him, and wedded his beautiful Anne, impoverished as she was. And now they were both dead; Anne in childbirth with the last child thirteen years before, the charming little girl who stared at him with her big, dark eyes as if he were an ogre, and Robert Ward in a carriage accident just this past month.

The boy suddenly put his arm around his little sister and murmured something to her. He was seventeen and the new heir, and although he was slim and downy-faced, already showed signs of growing into as handsome a man as his father had been before him. The property and inheritance, such as it was, had been left in trust to his aunt, the middle-aged lady in the wing chair, and Mr. Bentley himself, until Master Rob should come of age. The lawyer thought this singular; why not a male relative, no matter how distant the connection, instead of this ineffectual older sister, Mrs. Cardell? He looked at the oldest daughter curiously. He had the feeling that it was Miss Melissa who ordered the affairs of the house, young as she was. Suddenly she seemed to come to a decision, for she turned to her brother and said, "Do you take Nancy to the kitchen for a hot drink, Rob. Aunt Cardell, if you will excuse us, I would like to talk to Mr. Bentley in private."

The lawyer raised an eyebrow at such highhandedness, but Mrs. Cardell rose obediently and followed the others from the room.

"Of course, my dear, as you say. So unsuitable for them . . . I did warn you . . . but you insisted they be present. . . ."

Her lachrymose tones died away as Miss Ward firmly shut the door. "Now, Mr. Bentley," she said, pulling up a straight chair to the desk, "we will finish this affair with no more roundaboutation, if you please!"

The lawyer looked at her doubtfully as she seated herself across from him. She was certainly a fine looking young woman, he thought. Taller than usual, and slim, but then so had her father been above average height, and she had his black curls and high complexion, as well as a straight little nose and a fine pair of dark fringed blue eyes. The only features that marred what could have been a truly exceptional beauty were her generous mouth and a determined chin, now ominously set. Somehow it seemed to make her appear older than her nineteen years. The lawyer sighed, but before he could speak she asked, "Did my father have no plan for us at all? Surely even *he* could not have been so careless as to leave us destitute!"

Mr. Bentley was shocked, and hastened to reassure her. "Of course not, Miss Ward, and you are not destitute! It is unfortunate that his untimely death has brought all this to a head at this time . . ."

Miss Ward interrupted him impatiently. "I think that perhaps if he had lived to a ripe old age, we would have been destitute, sir!"

The lawyer looked at her strangely. What an unusual way to feel about a beloved parent, he thought, and she seemed to be aware of his disapproval.

"Yes, yes, I know. Hardly the most filial of statements, but then you see, even as I loved him dearly, I knew my father as well as you did. He was handsome and charming, gay and lovable, but he was also impractical and foolish, wild and heedless! I had no illusions about him, and if I did, they would have been speedily dispersed by the reading of his will, and your subsequent rendering of our accounts." She waved her hand around the library. "I have lived here all my life, sir, and seen how it has deteriorated. I knew we were in bad straits, but I never thought he would not have provided for his children in some way, and of course his sister, who has been dependent on him for years!"

Mr. Bentley oddly felt called upon to defend his late client. "As to that, Miss Ward," he said tartly, "he hardly expected to die at the age of forty-four!"

"More the pity he did not put his affairs in better order then!" she retorted quickly, and then added in a softer tone, "Oh, dear, I am sorry! That was unkind of me, wasn't it, to be raking poor Papa over the coals! He could not help being the way he was, but how are we to manage? How can Rob keep up Wardley Hall when he comes of age? And what of Nancy's debut? You notice I do not mention my own—that is clearly impossible! But what can I do to put things in order for them?"

If Mr. Bentley thought it singular that a nineteen-year-old girl should think herself capable of taking on such a burden, he made no mention of it. Instead he cleared his throat, determined to make the situation even clearer. "There is no way to put it in order, my dear Miss Ward. This has gone beyond remedy.

Even if you lived frugally it would not help. Oh, you will not starve, of course, but the estate is ruined."

Melissa frowned. "There is nothing to sell? No land left beyond this estate? Whatever happened to the property in Cornwall, and the one in Wells?" The lawyer sadly shook his head. "They are gone?"

"Sold long ago, I'm afraid," he admitted. "What is left is this house and the home farm, both sadly encumbered."

"Are you suggesting we must sell Wardley Hall?" Melissa asked softly in disbelief. "What inheritance then would Rob come into?"

The lawyer had had enough. He picked up his papers and put them in a folder as he said, "Miss Ward, let us not be premature. I will study the matter and return at a later date. There may be other assets ... in any event, there is no need for immediate haste. And now I fear I must be on my way if I hope to reach London before dark. I do not wish to travel on the Heath at night, not with all the instances of highwaymen as we have had lately!"

Melissa rose reluctantly, remembering to be polite. "I thank you, sir, for coming to us so promptly, and I shall look forward to seeing you again, when you have a complete list of our assets, if any, and debts—of which I am afraid there will be a great number!"

She shook the lawyer's hand firmly, and walked with him to the front door. Prims, the butler, was nowhere in sight which did not surprise her for she knew he always slept at this time of day in order to recoup his strength for serving dinner. Prims was elderly and doddering and should have been pensioned off long ago. His wife was not much better, although she continued to use the title "housekeeper" in a house that needed a lot more keeping than she was able to provide, old and arthritic as she was. A great deal of the work fell to Melissa and her aunt, and a small maid named Aggie. Between them, they managed.

After she had bade the lawyer farewell, Melissa stood indecisively in the hall for a few moments. She had no desire to rejoin the rest of the family, she was so stunned by Mr. Bentley's revelations. She looked blindly around the familiar shabbiness, and then she shook her head a little and ran lightly up the stairs to the privacy of her own room. Quickly she removed the ugly black dress that had been hastily remodeled from her aunt's wardrobe, and dropped it and her petticoats on the floor. She took her habit and riding boots from the clothes press. The habit was old and a little snug—not that there was any chance she could have a new one, she thought bitterly as she fastened the buttons and stamped her feet into the boots. Glancing in her mirror, she saw she would have to brush her hair again. Her curls seemed to have a mind of their own; no matter how severely she arranged them, before long they escaped the ribbon and tangled every which way. She frowned at her reflection as she pulled them back and pinned them up securely. Her big blue eyes stared back at her, dark with worry and anger. How could her dear, handsome father have been so careless of the future? Shaking her head again, she took up her crop and riding gloves and left the room. As she opened a side door, she saw that the weather was fast deteriorating. It had been a lovely summer morning, but now, as if in response to her mood, the sky was clouding over, and there would be rain before dark. She went through the neglected gardens and down to the stables without seeing anyone. She imagined Simon, the old groom, had gone to his cottage to work in the vegetable garden. As she saddled her mare she was glad Posie was so old, for there could be no question of selling her. She looked around at the other horses. At the moment the big stable was almost empty, although there were a pair of elderly carriage horses, Nancy's pony and Rob's mare, and her father's hunters and magnificent gelding, Captain. He whinnied to her, and she sighed as she realized that he at least would have to be sold, and the hunters too, in spite of the fuss Rob would make. Her frown deepened. She did not like to admit it to herself, but she saw signs in Rob that showed he had much the same character as his father. He never seemed to understand why, when he wrote for money, it was not immediately forthcoming, and all her lectures did not seem to do any good. Her father had laughed at her and said the boy had expenses at school, and a reputation to maintain. Well, now, Melissa thought grimly, things would have to be different, and Master Rob was going to be brought speedily to reality at last. Suddenly she came to a decision, and stripped the saddle off Posie. If Captain had to be sold, at least she could ride him until the unhappy event took place. Standing on a box, she put the saddle on his huge back. She had no fear of Captain for she had ridden him many times, and he could go like the wind. That was what she needed now, not a gentle amble on old Posie. She smiled as she remembered how her father had always claimed she was the best horseman in the family, including himself. She led the horse from the stable and over to the mounting block. Although he was restless from not being exercised lately, he stood patiently for her, almost as if he were aware she could not mount without the block. Soon they were trotting from the yard, heading for the fields surrounding the Hall.

Although only nineteen, Melissa Ward today felt twice that age with the weight of the worries and responsibilities she carried. Her father had often called her "My Guilty Conscience" or "Miss Practicality," and grinned at her as he said it, to remove the sting. She noticed it was Nancy who made his eyes light up, and had early decided that no one was overly fond of a conscience.

Sometimes she felt almost part of another family, so different she was from the rest. She could barely remember her mother, but she had heard enough tales of her frivolity, and what with her gay father, her wasteful brother, and her unconcerned little sister, only Aunt Cardell sympathized with her at all. She urged Captain to a canter, and resolved to put her troubles from her mind, for the next hour at least.

When she returned to the stable yard, Simon was there, and he took the horse from her as she dismounted.

"Aha! Captain, is it, Miss Lissa?" he asked with a grin. "Did ye know he threw Master Rob this week?"

Melissa had not, but it wasn't surprising that Rob had not regaled them with that piece of news. "He won't throw me!" she retorted. "He was as gentle as a lamb!"

"Aye, Captain knows who's who!" Simon chuckled as he led him away.

A few drops of rain were beginning to fall as she walked up to the Hall. How she loved Wardley! It stood on a slight rise, surrounded by terraces and gardens. She knew the tiles on the roof needed repairs, there was a loose shutter on one of Aunt

Cardell's windows, and the gardens were overgrown and neglected, but in the misty light the bricks of the facade were softened to old rose, and the Hall seemed to regain its charm and magnificence and appeared as it had always been. Wardley Hall! To save it she would do anything she had to without counting the cost!

She was in no hurry to go inside, so she strolled up and down the garden paths, ignoring the rain and thinking hard about what she must do now. There was no money; that was the heart of the problem, so somehow they had to *get* money. She wished she had thought to ask the lawyer if Rob's school fees were paid up. With summer coming she did not have to worry about it right away, but what about next year? Surely there was enough money for that! She frowned and switched the head from an innocent daisy with her crop. Of course there was plenty of food, from their own kitchen garden and the home farm. Because they were in mourning, there was no need for new clothes, although there would be by winter. Rob would have to be outfitted as befitted a gentleman's son, and with Nancy growing like a weed, she would need new clothes too. Well, Nancy at least could make do with hand-me-downs, and fortunately Aunt Cardell was an excellent seamstress.

Now, how do we get money, she asked herself, determined to be practical. There were no relatives that she knew of except her mother's family, as poor as they were. Her mother's sister had married well, but there had been a quarrel; about what she had never heard, for they had not communicated for as long as she could remember. She must be sure to suggest that Aunt Cardell write to the lady though, informing her of Robert Ward's death, she reminded herself. If worse came to worse, she could send Nancy to Aunt Alice. It might not be a happy life, but she wouldn't want for anything. Her father and aunt were children of an only child, so no wealthy aunts or uncles could be counted on from that side of the family. Rob had to finish school, it would be terrible to drag him away now! And to do what, she asked herself, clerk in an office? Help on the farm? She smiled broadly for the first time in days, imagining her brother in an eye shade, stoically toting up a long column of figures with inky fingers, or sweating and sunburned, driving a plow. Not Rob! She squared her shoulders and decapitated a dandelion. No, it was plainly up to her to get the money— somehow! She remembered the novels she had read. Clearly the easiest way would be for her to meet a fabulously wealthy old man and marry him. And, she thought ironically, have him drop dead on his wedding night, early on his wedding night! Perhaps drinking a last toast to his young bride. Ha! Two more daisies lay at her feet. The problem to this fanciful solution was that she didn't know any wealthy old men; in fact she didn't know any men wealthy or otherwise who weren't already married. Of course there was Jack. Jack Holland was her own age and had been her best friend from childhood, and although he would inherit his father's property someday, could hardly be called a prospect. The Hollands were comfortably off, but they did not have the money needed to restore Wardley. Furthermore, the squire would never give his consent for his nineteen-year-old heir to marry, even if she could get Jack to agree to the scheme. She could imagine his hoots of laughter if she were ever so silly as to suggest it. If

only she had enough money to get to London she was
sure to find a rich husband, but she didn't even have
enough for that.

The rain began to fall more heavily, and she gave
up her speculations for the moment and hurried into
the house. As she was changing out of her habit for
dinner, she looked at herself critically in the mirror.
Her black curls had escaped their ribbon again, and
clustered around her face, now rosy from her ride.
She attempted to put them in a sophisticated style,
wishing for perhaps the hundredth time that they
were guinea gold instead of plain black. Then she
tried smiling coyly at her reflection. It was no use;
she didn't have the flirtatious, tempting manner
that was surely a necessity for catching wealthy
husbands. Her reflection frowned back at her. She
had never given her face much thought, but Papa
had called her beautiful more than once. She
smoothed her hands over her faded gown. She had a
good figure, she thought, turning this way and that
and admiring her high breasts and slim waist. In a
more attractive gown . . . suddenly she stamped her
foot impatiently. No matter how she reasoned, it all
came back to marriage, the only resort for a girl in
1814. It was a depressing prospect, for she had
always thought she could marry only where she
loved, when she had thought about it at all.

Dinner was an unusually silent meal, although
Aunt Cardell tried to appear normal for Nancy's
sake, and Melissa chatted lightly with Rob until
Prims removed the pudding dishes. She excused the
butler, saying he did not need to clear the table yet.
Rob had been about to rise, and now he turned and
stared at her.

"Do you think this is quite the time, Lissa?" he

asked. "Nancy is worn out; perhaps after she goes to bed . . ."

"No, Nancy is part of the family, and she is thirteen now." Melissa smiled reassuringly at her younger sister to calm the fright in her big dark eyes. "I think we had all better discuss what is to be done, and since it will naturally concern Nancy, we should hear her thoughts too."

Nancy sat up a little straighter, and said earnestly, "Well, I am not sure I have any, Lissa, thoughts I mean, but I will try!"

"Good girl!" Aunt Cardell said gruffly.

Melissa folded her hands and frowned down at them. "I wish we had thought to ask Mr. Bentley about your school fees, Rob. If they are paid up, at least we don't have to worry about that for next year."

Rob stared across the table at her, his face white. "Paid or not, Lissa, the money must be found! Lord, a fine gentleman I'd make without schooling!"

"I think if some solution is not discovered, there won't be any question of being 'gentlemanly' or not!" Melissa retorted. "You may have to go to work."

"Work?" Rob asked in a horrified voice. "Surely you are funning! Things have not come to that pass yet; mark my words, old Bentley will find the money. These lawyers are all alike, full of doom and economy, but you've only to be firm with them and they come up with the ready!"

Melissa stared hard at her brother. "We really won't know until Mr. Bentley gives us some indication of the real state of our finances. There isn't any 'ready' though, Rob, however you'd like to think it! We must be extremely careful with the little we have, that is why I wanted to talk this over with everyone. Father's horses will have to be sold; I must ask Simon how we go about that. . . ."

"Now just a minute!" Rob exclaimed, his adolescent voice cracking strangely. His face grew whiter as he continued, "Those horses are mine now, and they will not be sold!"

"The horses are held in trust, as is the rest of the estate, Rob, and if Mr. Bentley and Aunt Cardell say they should go, go they must."

Rob turned to his aunt and asked hotly, "You wouldn't do such an infamous thing, would you, Aunt?"

Mrs. Cardell looked extremely uncomfortable. Much as she agreed with Melissa, she had a soft spot for her nephew. "Well, Rob," she said finally, nervously pleating her napkin, "we must see what is best. It really seems like poor economy to have them eating their heads off, with no one to ride them . . ."

"*I* will ride them, of course!" Rob interrupted.

Aunt Cardell brightened. "To be sure, my dear, you will." Then her smile faded. "But . . . but, when you go back to school perhaps then they had better be sold."

Rob opened his mouth to reply as Nancy piped up. "I should hate to lose Blossom, but you may sell her if you need, Lissa!"

Melissa got up and impulsively hugged her sister. "There is no need for you to give up your pony, Nancy, but it was generous to offer!"

Rob flushed. "I suppose you think I'm selfish! Well, I don't care! I have a certain standard to maintain, and I will not be reduced to one mare!"

Melissa whirled and glared at him. "Listen to me well, Rob! All this talk about 'gentlemen' and 'standards' is doing us no good at all. Don't you understand that we are in a fair way to being ruined? If money is not found, we may have to sell Wardley Hall! That we must avoid at all costs! I quite see you must finish school, but let us hear no more silly talk about 'standards!' " Her voice was rich with scorn, and Rob lowered his eyes. "Since we are in mourning, there is no question of entertaining this summer, or your going on a visit to friends, so the question is really of no consequence. What would be more to the point is for you to help on the farm so that at least your sisters and aunt will have enough to eat!"

Aunt Cardell broke in quickly, before Rob could reply. "Come, my dears, do stop pulling at each other! Yes, I see you are worried, Lissa, well, and so you should be! That brother of mine . . . I wish I had him here right now, I'd give him a piece of my mind! Oh, dear!" She suddenly crumbled and dissolved into tears, and Nancy hurried around the table to hug her. Melissa was ashamed of herself. It really could have been left till later when everyone's sorrows and tears had had a chance to abate. She rose and tried to smile.

"You are right, Aunt! We can discuss this some other time. But Rob, there must be no running up of bills! Let us agree that if a purchase is necessary, we will have a family council. Will you agree to that?"

She looked carefully at her brother as he threw down his napkin and rose, pushing his chair back so violently it almost fell.

"I will certainly be as prudent as I think necessary, but I will not be dictated to by a pack of females about *my* property!"

Before Melissa could speak, he rushed out of the dining room.

"Oh, dear," she said ruefully, "I have got his back

up, haven't I? Nancy love, run along and tell Prims
he can come and clear now." She waited until her
sister had left, and then said soberly to her aunt, "I
think it is going to be a rough road for us, Aunt,
bringing Master Rob to his senses. Good heavens, if
he is going to play Lord-of-the-Manor every time we
try to discuss it!"

Aunt Cardell patted her hand. "I know, Lissa, but
he is very young, remember, and this has all been a
shock to him. Be patient, and try not to order him
about. I am afraid you do not handle him the right
way!"

She was still talking about it as they made their
way to the drawing room where Melissa lit two work
candles so they might get on with the mending.
Nancy returned and settled down with a book, thereby
bringing Aunt Cardell's rambling advice to an end,
for that evening at least.

CHAPTER 2

The Young Gentleman's First Appearance

The next morning was filled with the usual chores, but finally Melissa escaped to the stables. Rob's mare was missing; he had gone out early that morning. Simon smiled warmly at her as he leaned on his shovel for he had just finished mucking out the stalls.

"Ah, Miss Lissa! Be ye riding today?"

Melissa gave him a hand with the barrow, for he was much too old for the heavy work he continued to do. "Yes, Simon, saddle Captain for me, if you please." She fed Posie a piece of apple so she wouldn't feel neglected while he prepared the gelding, and then she said, "I fear we must think of selling Captain, Simon, and the hunters too."

"It's like that, is it?" the old groom asked sharply, looking up from the stirrups he was adjusting. "Well, I suspicioned it might be! The master went his own road for many a day, but there had to be a reckonin'! We all comes to it at last!"

"We won't do anything quite yet, Simon . . . there may be a way out of it, but if worse comes to worst, I'll need your help in selling them for a good price."

Simon shook his head. "Weel, you'll need go no farther than the squire's to sell Captain! He's had 'is eye on 'im for many a day! I'll do all I can to help you, Miss Lissa!" he said fervently.

Melissa accepted his hand up, and picked up the reins. Her eyes were damp as she smiled down at the old groom. "I know I can count on you, Simon, you're a good friend!"

She rode out of the yard, blinking her eyes, although she knew Simon's eyesight was too poor for him to notice her distress. Riding towards Blackwood she hoped she would see Jack for she felt she had to talk to someone freely. As she trotted along the road, she could tell immediately when she reached the boundaries of the squire's property, it was in so much better order than Wardley Hall. It gave Melissa a pang every time she saw the well-drained ditches and neat fields, and the tenant farmers' cottages gleaming with fresh whitewash. Squire Holland kept his estate the way Wardley used to be kept. She sighed, and then, spying Jack in one of the fields, turned Captain through an open farm gate and rode towards him. He was speaking to one of the men, but he broke off abruptly when he caught sight of her and rode to meet her, calling as he came, "Lissa! Well met!"

She smiled at him. Jack Holland was a tall, fair young man with the easy, open manners of an old friend. Although no one would ever characterize him as needle-witted, Melissa always felt comfortable pouring out her troubles to him. Mrs. Holland had tried to get her husband to keep them apart in later years, for she wanted no son of hers marrying a Ward, even if they had been neighbors forever, but the Squire had only laughed at her.

"No need for such tactics, m'dear! Worse thing you could do, pon rep! Haven't you seen they're just like brother and sister, right down to the spats they have? Let 'em alone! Melissa won't marry Jack!" Beyond the obvious disparity of their birth, for the Wards were quality, no matter how impoverished, there was also the fact that Melissa was much too acute and intelligent for Jack, but the squire wisely did not point this out to the young man's fond mama.

Mrs. Holland sincerely hoped her husband was right, but privately looked forward to the day when Jack would go to London for a season as his father had promised he could do as soon as he reached an age where he could be depended upon to behave himself and not get into too many silly scrapes. In the meantime he spent his time profitably and happily learning how to manage the estate that would one day be his.

The two friends rode side by side for a while in companionable silence. Then Melissa said suddenly, "Jack, let's go up to Byway Brook. I must talk to you!"

He looked sideways at her, and seeing the frown on her face, made no mention of the fact that he was supposed to ride to the village on an errand for his father. When they reached the brook, one of their favorite spots, he helped Melissa to dismount, and tied their horses to a branch. Melissa sat down on a boulder and sighed, ignoring the panoramic view that included not only the neighboring fields and woodlands, but the thatched roofs of the village below.

"What's to do, Lissa? You look as serious as an owl!" Jack said as he stretched out in the grass beside her. Melissa plucked a grass stem and chewed it thoughtfully.

"I guess I do, but oh, Jack, I'm so worried! Father's lawyer was at the Hall yesterday, and things are in worse case than even I thought!" Gloomily she told him what the lawyer had said, finishing up with "so you see, I must think of some way to get money—a lot of money!"

"But how?" asked Jack, who was nothing if not blunt. "How can a nineteen-year-old girl get money?"

"I don't know exactly, but I see it is clearly up to me. Aunt Cardell is no use, Nancy is too young, and Rob won't help!"

"Well, to be fair, Lissa, Rob's too young too!" Jack told her.

"But what can I do? Governesses only earn a pittance, barely enough to support themselves, but what other way is there for a girl to make money? I have quite decided that I must marry as soon as I can, and to a very wealthy man!"

Jack looked startled. "What wealthy man?"

"That's the problem, I don't know any! But if I had enough money, I could go to London and meet one. . . ."

Jack laughed heartily. "And how would you go about that? Walk up to men on the streets and ask to see their bank balance? Lord, Lissa, what a foolish plan! Besides, have you thought . . . I mean . . . you probably wouldn't like to be married, just for money!" He looked down, blushing fiercely.

Melissa sighed again. "I know, I'll hate it! But I shall just have to become accustomed to it for the family's sake. I daresay it won't be too bad once I get used to it. After all, lots of girls marry men they

don't know particularly well." Her voice died away
as she considered this awful prospect. To her surprise, Jack did not try to dissuade her again.

He was thinking hard, and it did seem to be the
only practical solution. Finally he said in a subdued
voice, "But do you have the money to go to London?
You'd have to hire a house and take Aunt Cardell
with you, and Nancy too. And seriously, Lissa, although a Ward may marry where she pleases, I have
the feeling it would be harder to meet society than
you think, without anyone backing you. And I don't
think you'd consider what my father calls a 'Cit' or a
'Nabob'! You would have to find someone of your
own kind who was also wealthy!"

"Well, there's Aunt Alice. I could write to her, my
aunt, Lady Throckmorton, I mean. We have never
met, but she might let me stay with her for the
season if I could provide my own clothes and not
cause her any expense, and surely she must move in
the best social circles. That way I wouldn't need a
house, or Aunt Cardell to lend me consequence. But
I quite see that I would need a large sum to buy
expensive clothes, and how to get that I don't know!"

"You know I would lend you any amount, Lissa,"
Jack said earnestly. "The fact is, m'father keeps me
on a pretty tight rein. . . ."

Melissa smiled at him. Dear Jack! He was a good
friend! "No, no, I wouldn't ask it of you! But there
must be some way; think hard, Jack!"

He knitted his brow in thought and stared at the
brook, bubbling away at their feet, while Melissa
absently began to make a daisy chain. Finally he
said, "It's too bad you're not a man; it's easier for
men to get money. In fact, my father was going on
only last night at dinner about highwaymen. It

seems they are more prevalent than ever, and Mr. Everett over to Whitesly was stopped just last week on the Heath and lost his purse with fifty guineas in it to one called 'Silent Simon.' " He sat up in boyish enthusiasm. "Wouldn't that be famous, Lissa? And I'd help! I bet we could get you a fortune in no time!" Suddenly he came back to earth. "Not that either of us would steal. That was silly of me, wasn't it?"

Melissa stared at him, her eyes sparkling with excitement. "Why is it silly? I don't call fifty guineas *silly!* I'd do anything to save Wardley Hall and I need the money too badly to worry about dishonesty! I wager I'd be a good highwayman! You know I'm an excellent rider, and you taught me to shoot yourself. And I know where my father's pistols are. . . ."

Jack held up his hands in alarm. "Wait a minute! I was only joking! You can't really be seriously considering it? It won't do; you're a girl!"

"Well, naturally I'd be masked, and wear an old coat. Who would know I was a girl if I put up my hair and covered it with a hat? In fact, simply because I *am* a girl would help; no one would ever suspect me! Besides, Captain can outride every horse in the county!"

"Aye, and he's known to everyone in the county too, even if he shows 'em all his heels. Lord, one holdup and they'd be knocking on your door within the hour! Give over, Lissa, do!"

She was silent, and Jack felt a great relief that he had convinced her this mad scheme was impossible.

"But what if I said I sold Captain?" Melissa went on slowly. "I could keep him in the stable at the old Welton farm on the edge of Wardley. No one has lived there for years, and no one goes there either since Grandma Welton hung herself. You know the farmers think she haunts the place. . . ."

Jack snorted, but he knew she was right, for wasn't it Melissa and himself who frightened two farmhands one early winter dusk by appearing draped in sheets near the farm? How they had laughed when the two ran for their lives!

Melissa continued, "I could ride Posie there at night and leave her until I return. No one would suspect a thing that way! Let's see, what else would I need?"

Jack was now extremely perturbed. He had said he would help Melissa and so he would, but this plan was sheer madness. And to think it had been his idea! He searched his mind desperately for a way to deter her before she swept them both up into disaster.

"Wait, Lissa! What if you get caught? What if one of the guards shoots you? Have you considered what they do to highwaymen? Maybe you haven't seen one after he's been hanged and drawn and quartered, but I have!"

"But I won't get caught," Melissa interrupted, cheerfully ignoring the gruesome picture he painted. "I'll only pick carriages that have a driver and no guards or outriders! Of course, I quite see that it will take longer that way, for surely if you were transporting a lot of money and valuables you would hire guards. And don't worry, I haven't any intention of getting you involved in this, I'll do it myself! I know every field and lane for miles around. Oh, Jack, I think you have hit on the very scheme, bless you!"

Jack groaned and buried his face in his hands. How could he let her go off on such a wild adventure alone? All their lives it had been Melissa who thought up the reckless plots and mad escapades, and he had been happy to follow her lead. But this! This was not a prank in the churchyard on All Hallows' Eve! The two friends were silent for many moments; Melissa looking for a flaw in her plans, and Jack trying to think of some way to dissuade her. As son of the district's justice of the peace, he often heard of criminal cases. He just hoped he never had to hear Melissa Ward's name mentioned in such a connection. Desperately, he tried one more time to stop her.

"Lissa! You must promise me not to do anything so foolish! It's just like you to go off half-cocked and get yourself shot the first time you try it!"

Melissa got up and stretched. "Oh, I won't do anything foolish, Jack. In fact there are so many details to think of, and it is such a serious step, I daresay I will end up giving up the scheme in the end!"

Jack was relieved. Surely when she had a chance to consider it she would see how impossible such a plan was. Even Melissa, as brave a girl as he had ever known, was not crazy enough to try anything so dangerous. He looked up at the sky.

"Look at the sun! I must hurry or I won't have a chance to get to the village before tea." The two friends hurried to the horses and in a few moments were on their way back to the road. Melissa chatted easily of estate matters until they parted. Jack once more warned her to be prudent then, and Melissa demurely agreed to do nothing rash as she turned Captain for home. If Jack had known the thoughts going through her head, he would not have felt so relieved and cheerful the rest of the day.

Melissa rode thoughtfully, barely seeing the way Captain took her. When Simon came out of the stable to hold the horse for her to dismount, she said casually, "I have been thinking that perhaps we should sell Captain first. Will he bring a good price, Simon?"

"Oh, aye, more than any o' them hunters, Miss Lissa!"

She nodded reflectively. "I see. Thank you, Simon." As she went back to the house, she considered the possibilities. Was it really such a mad idea then? She could think of no other solution to her problems, and if she were very careful, perhaps . . .

Rob had meant to ignore her that evening at dinner, to show her how displeased he was with her managing ways, but he found that she paid him no attention. Even Aunt Cardell looked at her sharply when she had to be spoken to twice. She went up to bed early, and before she slept, she went to her father's room and removed his silver-chased dueling pistols and some powder and shot, and hid them in an old band box at the back of her closet. If Rob asked for them, she would say that Father must have sold them. It was a small step, but it seemed to mark the beginning of the adventure, and she went to sleep more easily than she had since the funeral.

All through the following days, the plan was never far from her thoughts. As she weeded the vegetables, carefully wearing gloves and a large brimmed hat to protect her complexion, she would hear a small voice inside her head say "mask"; or again, while folding sheets, the same voice would remind her, "cloak." She wrote nothing down, but she returned to her father's room more than once to search for the things she needed. At the same time, she was often assailed by doubts. It *was* wrong to steal; not for nothing had she sat all those years in

the Wardley pew at church and listened to the vicar
preach on the commandments, but she continued to
plan nevertheless. Some days she was sure she would
never go through with it, but on other days she
would toss her black curls and decide that her need
was greater than the people she intended to rob.
What would they do with the money but spend it on
gambling and fripperies? And she had no intention
of robbing anyone who couldn't spare it, aye, and
more besides! She said nothing more about selling
the horses, or practicing even more stringent econ-
omies, and Rob was relieved. He did try to help when
he thought of it, but more often he rode off early and
was gone till dinner time. Aunt Cardell was worried
about him, but she did not know how to question
him without getting him in a towering rage. Even as
a small boy he had been able to intimidate her with
his temper tantrums, and she was glad Melissa left
him alone, for her intervention would surely have
precipitated a major storm. She often wondered what
on earth the girl had on her mind, so quiet as she
had become, but she welcomed the peace it brought
nevertheless. Nancy was the quietest of all, for she
missed her father sorely. Everyone was kind to her,
and the squire and Mrs. Holland regularly included
her in riding expeditions and shopping trips, and
invited her to spend days at Blackwood where she
could be with her friend Joan, Jack's youngest sister.

Mr. Bentley posted down from town again, and
although things were not as black as Melissa had
imagined, there was no money to spare. Rob would
be able to finish school, and he gave some money to
Aunt Cardell for the immediate household expenses,
but that was all the luxury they were allowed.
Melissa had the wild thought of asking him to lend

her enough money so she could go to London in search of a wealthy husband, but her courage failed her. Surely he would think her much too coming if she proposed such a scheme! He reminded Melissa that she had not notified her aunt of her father's death, and she was ashamed that such an important letter had not been sent. As soon as the lawyer took his leave, she sat down with Aunt Cardell to write the Throckmortons. It was easier than she had imagined, for they decided not to ask for any help, and merely said that Robert Ward was dead, and the family continued at Wardley Hall for the present. It would be wonderful if Aunt Alice hurried to Wardley and showered them with largesse, but Melissa had small hopes of it. When Aunt Cardell told her that Mr. Bentley had left the family some thirty pounds for expenses, a little devil in her head told her that if she had held him up on the way, she would be that much richer by now, and he would have had to send for more! He had come in a hired job-chaise, with only a driver and no guard.

One evening in late July when she knew Rob was dining with a friend's family, and Nancy was spending the night at Blackwood, she rode Captain over to the deserted farm. She had been there many times before in the gig when she could get away, taking oats and hay and all the necessary equipment she would need to stable the horse there. She half expected Simon to say something for he must have noticed the missing tack, but he never mentioned it to her relief. She had cleaned up the old stable as best she could, glad there was still a good roof on it. This evening she waited until Simon left the stable, and then saddled Captain and Posie, and leading the mare, made her way cautiously to the farm. She went out

of her way to avoid the better traveled lanes and was
fortunate not to see anyone, not even in the distance.
She unsaddled Captain, talking soothingly to him
while she brushed him down. After watering him
well, and filling the hayrack with a generous measure of oats, she left him. He did not seem to be upset
by his new surroundings, although she reminded
herself to bring a couple of the barn cats back with
her on the morrow. Such a deserted stable was sure
to have its resident rats and mice, and she could not
afford to lose Captain's oats and corn, they were too
hard to supply. She rode home through the warm
summer dusk triumphantly. At last she had really
begun, and now she had taken such an irrevocable
step, she felt she was well on her way to success.

After dinner, as she and her aunt sat in the
drawing room waiting for the tea tray and working
on the seemingly endless pile of mending, she told
Aunt Cardell that she had sold Captain and sent the
money to Mr. Bentley to invest for them. Her aunt
looked at her sharply as she bent her head over her
sewing again.

"Are you sure you have done the right thing,
Lissa?" she asked timidly. "Rob will be so angry!"

"I know he will, but it had to be done, and I got
such a good price for him! Jack Holland told me
about this man, and I did not dare delay any longer.
Rob will get over it, and we still have the hunters for
him." She snipped her thread serenely and folded
the petticoat of Nancy's that she had been working
on. She had no fear that her aunt would question
Jack or Simon for she had no reason to be suspicious.
Even if Rob should query Simon he would gain
nothing from it, for Melissa intended to speak to him
before she told her brother anything, and she knew

Simon would back her up. She had always been his favorite, from the time she had insisted he lift her up onto one of her father's horses, at age six. Robert Ward had been furious when he saw her and would have dismissed Simon then and there, but Melissa had cried, "I made him do it, Papa! See me ride!" and she had tried to kick the horse into motion. Her father had burst out laughing at her, so tiny and furious because she could not get the huge animal to move, and had forgiven Simon at once.

She smiled at her aunt now, for she still looked worried. "Do not fret, dear! I will tell Rob tomorrow, and he'll only be angry for a little while!"

It worked out just as she had planned, although she had more trouble with Simon than she thought.

"Sold Captain, Miss Lissa?" he asked sharply, peering closely at her. "Who bought him? And 'ow did you 'ear about it? I thought you wuz going to arsk me when you got ready to let 'im go!" He seemed more affronted by the fact that he had been left out of the transaction than suspicious of how it had happened.

"Jack Holland told me of this Mr. . . . er . . . Wilson!" she said soothingly. "He was willing to pay as much as the squire, and since I couldn't bear to let him go to the Hollands where I would be sure to see him often, I thought it best to sell him away." That had been a stroke of inspiration, for Simon knew how she loved the gelding, and he nodded his head. "If Rob should question you, just tell him you know nothing about it! I don't want him to be angry at you!"

"Nay, don't be afeared o' that, Miss Lissa! I wish it didn't 'ave to be, that's all!" Shaking his head sadly, the old man turned back to his chores, and Melissa went up to the Hall to get the interview with her brother over quickly. She missed the speculative look that Simon gave her as she hurried away.

Rob went white and clenched his fists when she told him that Captain was gone, but he knew he was powerless, and merely asked for some of the money from the sale for his expenses. When Melissa told him she had sent it all to Mr. Bentley, he was furious, and raged at her. When he accused her of trying to keep him penniless so he would have to stay home, she lost her temper too, and in a few moments they were engaged in the sort of loud argument they had often had as children. Aunt Cardell hurried to the library and clapped her hands in dismay. She was looking so distraught and trembly that Melissa was ashamed of herself, and went to put her arms around her. While she was soothing her, Rob left the room, slamming the door behind him.

Melissa stared at it, and then said softly, "Sometimes I wonder why I bother. If it were only for Nancy and you, dear Aunt, I would not judge any sacrifice too hard, but to put myself out for Rob when he won't even try! It does go against the grain with me!"

She realized she had said too much when her aunt began to question her, and had to invent a story about her activities before she was free to escape to her room. Aunt Cardell was so upset about the quarrel and her fears about Rob that it was easier than it should have been. She did not worry about Melissa, but she was more troubled about Rob and Nancy than she cared to admit. They seemed to be taking their father's death so hard!

That evening as Melissa stared idly out the window after dinner, she realized there was no longer any reason why she should not begin her new career.

It was a bright moonlight night, perfect for her first attempt as a highwayman. She shivered a little and bit her thumbnail as she considered it. Part of her wanted to wait; to be sure that everything was perfect, that she had forgotten nothing in her planning, but another side of herself murmured 'faintheart! You have to start sometime!' Turning from the window, she resolved to do it that very night. Nancy went to bed early, worn out from her day at the Hollands, but Melissa thought that Aunt Cardell would never fold up her embroidery and stop chatting, or Rob take himself off to bed. Eventually everyone took their candles and went upstairs. Melissa locked her bedroom door and changed quietly to the breeches and loose shirt she had found in her father's room and altered to fit. She pulled her black curls back ruthlessly and fastened them securely under a large brimmed hat. When she caught a glimpse of herself in the mirror she was startled! Surely no one would ever expect this was Melissa Ward, she looked so different! After she had checked the pistols to be sure they were loaded, and made certain she had her mask and greatcoat ready, she blew out her candle, pulled back the curtains to let the moonlight stream into the room, and sat down to wait for what seemed like an age until there was no sound of activity in the house. At last she rose and tiptoed out of her room and down the stairs, cautiously avoiding the creaking step halfway down that she knew could betray her. She held the coat and pistols in one hand and her boots in the other, and it was so awkward, she decided to leave some of them at the farm after this so she wouldn't have so much to carry. She let herself out of the side door, carefully leaving it unlatched. The horses whinnied as she crept into the stable, but she felt safe from discovery now. It had been a long time since Wardley Hall had stableboys who slept in the loft, and Simon was undoubtably snoring in his cottage some distance away. She soon had Posie saddled. The mare seemed puzzled and kept trying to nuzzle her as she led her to the mounting block. Melissa patted her soothingly and spoke softly until she seemed to accept the idea of a ride this late at night. Only then did Melissa mount and turn Posie's head towards the distant farm. She met no one, nor did she expect to. The farm laborers were all asleep after a hard day in the fields, and the track was deserted. It seemed as bright as day, and she thanked God for the moonlight as she rode along. When she reached the farm, she put Posie in the stall next to the gelding, leaving her saddled. She did not know how much time she would have when she returned, and if she were chased, it was important she be back in the Hall as soon as possible. Captain seemed glad to see her and stamped an impatient hoof as she saddled him and adjusted the stirrups. "Hush, Captain!" she murmured to him. "You will soon have a chance to gallop as fast as you like!"

She strapped the greatcoat and pistols behind the saddle and mounted, and then she set Captain to a walk until they gained the lane. She held him to a canter for a while, but as they approached the postroad she kicked him to a gallop. She wanted to shake the restlessness out of him before they reached their destination; a copse she had chosen earlier that had a good view of the road in both directions. After a few miles when she was sure he would not betray them with a whinny or the sound of restless hooves as they waited, she reined him in, and bending forward, patted his neck. "Good boy! Now if only you won't shy as I fire!"

They seemed to reach the copse much sooner than she had expected. She went on to the next turn in the road and carefully scanned the highway. There was no one in sight, so she rode back and turned Captain aside past the tall grass at the roadside and in amongst the trees. It seemed dark there in the shadows after the brilliance of the moonlit road, and she was sure she could not be seen. She had picked this location with care; it was not too far from home and there were no farms or villages nearby. Several paths offered escape routes and would make it difficult for any pursuer to know which way she had gone. She slid from Captain's back and tethered him to a tree before she loosened the bundle behind the saddle. It seemed a very warm night to be wearing a greatcoat, she thought as she shrugged into it, but she dared not go without it for she was not at all sure that the loose shirt hid her breasts sufficiently. The mask took longer; her fingers seemed curiously wooden as she tried to knot it, and she was perspiring when she finally secured it so only her eyes showed. It clung to her mouth and she blew at it impatiently. There was certainly more to this than she had thought! She felt hot and uncomfortable as she put the loaded pistols gingerly in her pockets and led Captain to a log so she could remount. Safely back in the saddle, she stuck one pistol in her belt and grasped the other as she settled down to wait. Captain stood patiently, merely shifting his weight now and then, although he pricked up his ears when an owl hooted nearby, startling both of them, and reared a little when a small animal ran close to his hooves. As she talked to him soothingly, she thought

that there was still time to call off the adventure.
After all, she was not committed as yet, and maybe
Jack was right and she would be shot, or caught and
exposed. She shrugged impatiently, her hands
clammy in the pigskin gloves, and the mask tickling
her nose. There was no other way, and this was
merely nerves, but she wished someone would come!
The waiting was the hardest part, and if she had to
tarry much longer she knew she would lose her
courage for it did seem to be getting very late! The
owl hooted again, and it was such a lonesome, eerie
sound that she wished she were back in her own
room, safely asleep in bed. She had never been out
alone at night, and the noises she heard disturbed
her more than they did Captain. Suddenly the sound
of hooves came faintly through the night. She leaned
forward eagerly and stared down the road in their
direction. She reminded herself that she must be
cautious and stop only an unaccompanied coach for
it would be the height of folly to try and take a
well-defended one, all by herself. As the hoofbeats
drew nearer, she realized there was only a single
horse approaching, and she retreated deeper into the
woods in disappointment. Captain stirred in response
as the solitary rider swept down the road towards
them and away. She watched him disappear and
hoped the coach she sought would not appear until
he was out of earshot, or he might ride back to
investigate. She did not relax until all sounds of
horse and rider had faded away. A long time ensued,
and she was about to give up in disgust and not some
little relief, when she again heard horses in the
distance. Sounds traveled further at night she realized, as she removed the glove from her right hand
and wiped the perspiration carefully away on her

coat. She needed a firm grip. She adjusted her mask which had slipped down a little, and made sure her hat was pulled well forward over her face, and only then did she move Captain ahead to a spot where she could see the road. It seemed an endlessly long time before an old traveling coach came lumbering around the bend. There was only a single driver, and no attendant outriders, and the coach was moving at a slow pace. This was it! She waited, her heart pounding hard until she judged they were close enough, and then she drew a deep breath and kicked Captain down the grass verge and into the road. The team drawing the coach halted abruptly and tried to rear as she fired her pistol off into the air.

"Stand and deliver!" she ordered in the gruffest voice she could manage. It came out more like a squeak, but fortunately no one seemed to notice. The coachman was wrestling with the frightened team, one of whom was tangled in the traces. She hastily put the used pistol in a pocket, and drawing the remaining pistol from her belt, edged closer.

" 'Ere, you!" she growled, more successfully this time. "Throw down your weapon or I fire!"

The coachman obeyed quickly, the blunderbuss sailing into the tall grass and out of sight.

"Now, get down outa there, and go to the 'orses 'eads!"

The elderly man obeyed as quickly as he could, and was soon holding the bridles steady. Melissa moved Captain to the door of the coach and flung it open. Cowering inside was a very fat elderly man in puce satin. He stared at the silver-chased pistol she pointed at him, and seemed to shrink in terror.

" 'And up your purse, my good man," she demanded, and was thrilled when he hastened to do so, muttering imprecations and threats at the same time. " 'Old your tongue! This 'ere pistol has an 'air trigger!" The mutters stopped abruptly. Melissa stowed the pouch of money in her pocket, and then she barked, "Off wiv your watch and chain, guv, and I'll have that fine ring you're sportin' too!"

The elderly man bristled as he removed his jewelry, and began to splutter again, his face turning even redder in his indignation. His complexion could not be said to enhance puce satin.

"What is to become of the world," he asked, "if a man cannot drive home from an evening party peaceably without being molested and robbed? And by a young boy, too, from what I can judge! 'Tis a disgrace!"

"Aye, that it is!" Melissa agreed cheerfully, as the jewelry followed the money pouch into her pocket, and she glanced at the coachman to be sure he was not trying to reach the gun. "And now I bid you good-evening, my dear sir," she said, dropping the common accent she had assumed. "My thanks for the heavy purse and the kickshaws. You can be sure that I will put them to better use than you would have!" She laughed and wheeled her horse, taking care to keep the pistol pointed somewhere between the coachman and her victim. "If anyone asks," she couldn't resist adding, "just you tell 'em that 'The Young Gentleman' was the culprit!" Suddenly she fired the other pistol over the horses' heads, causing them to rear and fight the coachman so he had his hands full as she made her escape. She kicked Captain hard and he needed no further urging as he galloped away down the road in the direction from which the coach had appeared. She wanted its bulk between her and the men in case they recovered the gun quickly. She went as fast as she dared and was soon around the bend and out of sight, and she thanked the bright moonlight again, for the lane she sought was poorly marked. When she had turned into it and ridden down it to the field she knew would allow her a shortcut home, she felt safer, and slowed Captain to a walk. Behind a large haystack she paused and listened hard. There was no sound of pursuit and she sighed in relief. It seemed to be the first breath she had taken since she rode out of the copse, and her hands were shaking in earnest now that she was out of danger. She waited until her heart slowed its beat, and then rode on for she knew she must reach home as quickly as possible. It seemed to take a long time before they reached the farm and she slid from Captain's back to lead him into his stall and hastily unsaddle him. She brushed him down quickly and fed him, and resolved to return tomorrow early and take better care of him. He had behaved beautifully, as if he were used to being on the high toby! She put the pistols in an old sack and hung them up with the greatcoat high on the wall, away from the rats, stowing her night's booty in Posie's saddlebags. She did not really relax until she slipped in the side door of Wardley Hall and crept up the stairs to her room. Lighting the candle with hands that still shook so she could hardly manage the flint, she turned the pouch out on the bed. The gold guineas poured out in a satisfying stream. The old gentleman must have had luck at the card table, she thought, as she counted them. Thirty-five guineas! Not bad for her first try, and the ring looked valuable too! The watch chain was mere frumpery, but the timepiece itself was solid gold, and heavy. She gathered everything up triumphantly and put the jewelry in the bandbox where she kept the powder and shot for the pistols. The money went into a locked chest with the few small pieces of jewelry she had inherited from her mother. She would have to find a safer place she reminded herself as she sleepily undressed and slid into bed. Even though she kept the key on a chain around her neck, Nancy was a curious child, and it wouldn't be too hard for her to force the lock. How could she possibly explain her hoard of guineas? She would take care of it tomorrow; she was so tired! As she drifted off to sleep, she heard an owl hoot again. Maybe it was the same one who had called in the copse as she waited for the coach, she remembered with a small smile, no longer frightened by the sound, and he had flown with her to see her safely home. It seemed like a good omen.

CHAPTER 3

The Duke Overhears an Interesting Conversation

Anthony St. Eustace Adams Northrup, the Duke of Colchester, strolled leisurely through the gardens of Blackwood, early the following afternoon. He had arrived the day before at the squire's invitation, for a few days' stay on his way back to London. His friends in the Corinthian set would have been amazed to see him consorting with a country squire and his family, but the duke was a familiar visitor. Squire Holland and Anthony's father had been at school together and rather unusually had continued their friendship long after they went their separate ways; the squire to the life of a country gentleman, and the duke to his vast estates, his magnificent London town house, and his considerable fortune. When young Anthony lost both his father and his mother to the fever when he was fifteen, the Hollands had taken pity on him and invited him to visit them as often as he pleased. He was an only child, and much preferred the easygoing ways of Blackwood to the formality of his own home, and the company of the Hollands to that of his army of servants and an elderly aunt and uncle. He had not seen much of Blackwood in recent years, for as he grew older and attained his majority, he spent more time in London during the season, pursuing all the pleasures available to a wealthy, handsome young man. He was twenty-eight, some nine years older than Jack whom he considered a young cub still. However, he paused when he heard the boy's voice coming from the gazebo in the center of the garden, for he had never heard that particular tone in Jack's voice before.

"Well, of all the crackbrained, crazy things to do! I never thought you'd be so foolish, Lissa! Insanity, that's what it is, insanity, and what if you'd been caught, you shatter-pated little idiot! A highwayman, indeed!"

The duke was intrigued, and moved closer as a girl's voice hushed him. "Do be quiet, Jack! The only way I am apt to get caught at this stage is if you continue to announce my adventure to the world! Do remember your father is justice for the county!"

Jack obediently lowered his voice, and the duke had to strain to hear his impassioned reply. "Yes, you absurd hoyden, and if you had been caught, you'd be standing before him even now, and then how do you think we'd all feel?"

"Well, I didn't, so why are you getting so excited?" There was a little pause, and then she continued, a bubble of laughter in her voice. "Oh, Jack, it was famous! I wish you might have seen me! 'Stand and deliver!' I cried in my lowest tones as I fired over the horses' heads. The coachman had so much to do controlling the team, he threw down his gun without a word! And the fat old beau inside! How you would have laughed at him! His eyes were all but popping from his head in fright! And I got thirty-five guineas and some very expensive jewelry."

Jack groaned and she continued, "You're just sorry you missed it! Truly, dear Jack, I was very careful, there was no danger at all!"

"Unless the old gentleman had had a pistol in the coach!" Jack retorted. "Oh, Lissa, give over! You cannot continue with it, I'll not let you! This is no prank, and there will be no mercy for you if you are caught!"

"Well, I am prepared to risk it. I would do *any-thing,* anything at all to save Wardley!" Melissa replied bravely. "And surely if I can get that much money in one night, it won't be long before I have enough to go to London and marry a fabulously rich man and all my problems will be solved! Surely a smart ball gown cannot cost more than fifty guineas."

The duke's eyebrows rose and he stifled a laugh at this ingenuous statement. In his mind's eye he saw the extraordinary bill for gowns that Mme Thérèse had presented to him recently. His latest demirep was not the frugal type and would have considered fifty guineas mere pin money. He wondered idly what this unusual young miss looked like, as she continued briskly.

"Now, Jack, I rode over because there is something you have to do that is very important! I didn't tell you before because I knew you would try and stop me, but now you must be sure to tell your father as soon as you can manage it, and in a very casual way you know, that we have sold Captain. I have him safe at the farm, but the old gentleman may have given a description of him. Tell your father that Simon sold him a week ago, to a man passing through the village." She considered for a moment. "No, not the village, it is so small that everyone knows when a stranger has been there. Tell him Simon took him to Washburn on market day last."

Jack agreed reluctantly. The astute lady highwayman then commanded, "Be sure and let me know if the old gentleman complains to your father of being robbed. I wager he will, and I am curious to know how he describes me! I told him I was called 'The Young Gentleman' after he deplored the customs and manners of modern youth!" Jack could not help a small chuckle at this. The duke prepared to move away as soon as he heard her add, "I must be gone! Aunt Cardell will be wondering what on earth has happened to me for I overslept this morning. There is a prodigious amount of waiting about in this game, I can tell you; it was hours before the coach came down the road! I don't think I was ever up so late before," she added naively.

"Hold, Lissa!" Jack's urgent voice came again. "When will I see you again? You're not planning another . . . er . . . holdup, are you?"

The duke heard her laugh. "No, Mr. Caution, at least not yet! I will contrive to meet you tomorrow— say, at Byway Brook about three? I cannot wait to hear if the old dandy files a complaint!"

The duke moved away hastily until he was screened from sight of the gazebo by Mrs. Holland's prize rhododendron hedge as he heard them making sounds of departure. He risked a quick look through the branches but saw nothing but the back of a shabby habit and a few black curls under a large hat as the girl rode away down the drive. He watched Jack come cautiously out of the gazebo, glance quickly around, and then stroll towards the house with such an air of innocence that he contrived to look the picture of guilt, as if he himself were the young highwayman! The duke admitted that the conversation he had just heard had piqued his interest. It was quiet at Blackwood, and he had been suffering a sense of *ennui* since his arrival, and wondering if perhaps he might be wise to cut his visit short. The truth was that Anthony Northrup was becoming bored with all aspects of his life. It seemed so futile—the visits to friends' estates, the hunting parties, the balls and routs and daily trips to his clubs when he was in town, the gambling and drinking till dawn, and the latest in a long line of pretty little light-skirts—none of these things had the power to bring anything more to his face than a slight smile or a stifled yawn. He was thoroughly spoiled if he could have but known it, by his wealth and position and the toadying and fawning that he had become accustomed to, and he was drifting without purpose into even more dissipation without anyone to say him nay. The squire had looked at him sharply on his arrival, concerned to see the weary eyes and the lines that had no place in a twenty-eight-year-old face, and had wondered uneasily if he should take Tony to task about it. He hoped at the very least to get him to spend a long time at Blackwood on a repairing lease.

The dissipated duke continued his stroll down to the stream that bordered the garden and considered what he should do about the extraordinary conversation he had just heard. What he should do, he well knew, was to tell the squire immediately, before the young lady came to grief. If she were stopped now it could all be kept quiet, a mere prank attributable to youthful high spirits, especially if the money and jewelry were returned to the rightful owner. It did not seem to distress him when he decided against this prudent course without the slightest hesitation, and he freely acknowledged that his lack of good intentions was not merely a disinclination to meddle, but stemmed from a strong desire to watch the farce unfold. Casually he wondered why she needed the money so badly. She had certainly not been of vulgar birth; that was obvious from her tone and accents. Suddenly he came to a decision, and walked back to the house more purposefully. Before going to change his clothes, he directed the butler to send a message to the stable, and not many minutes passed before he turned his horse down the drive and rode gently in the direction the lady highwayman had taken.

When he returned some hours later, he assured Mrs. Holland he had spent a pleasant afternoon visiting some old haunts he remembered from his visits as a child, and regaled her with an account of the people he had met in the village, but he neglected to mention that he had carefully inspected as much of Wardley Hall as he had been able to see from the overgrown drive, and had spent some time in conversation with an elderly pensioner out weeding his garden on the outskirts of the property, under the guise of asking for a cold drink of water.

When the family gathered for dinner that evening, the squire came bustling in, quite late. His wife clucked reprovingly to him, and he hastened to explain to his guest.

"My dear Tony! A thousand pardons, my boy! If you were not quite one of the family I would feel even worse for deserting you this way. To tell the truth, I have been detained by an interview with a Mr. Colbert who was robbed last night on the post-road." He sat down and shook out his napkin, as Tony glanced at Jack. The young man was bent over his soup, but a flush of color stained his cheeks. The duke smiled at his host.

"Think nothing of it, my dear sir! I take it the neighborhood is being plagued by some highwayman? 'Tis almost an insult, so close to the home of the justice, is it not?"

The squire snorted. "Aye, and what I'd give to get my hands on him, the young rascal!"

"Young?" Tony inquired gently. "There was such a good description?"

"Mr. Colbert said it was a youth, a mere boy! And he had the gall to name himself 'The Young Gentleman'!"

Jack spoke up casually, his flush now died away. "What did the young man look like, Father, did he say?"

"Oh, as to that, he was heavily masked and cloaked. 'Twas only his voice and the slightness of his frame that led Mr. Colbert to guess his age. I have not heard of any such person before; perhaps he is a stranger passing through. If, however," he added grimly, "he continues his activities around here, he will be quickly apprehended!"

A small devil caused the duke to inquire further. "Was there a description of his horse, Squire?"

Jack's soup spoon clattered slightly against his plate as his father answered. "Why, yes, a large black gelding. The only horse that comes immediately to mind like that is Robert Ward's Captain, which further strengthens my suspicion the thief is a stranger to the district."

Jack raised his napkin as he began to cough, and the conversation came to an abrupt halt until the spell was over. Mrs. Holland fussed over her son, telling him not to eat so fast, and when silence was restored and the servants had presented the next course, a new topic of conversation was introduced. When the butler had removed the covers, and Mrs. Holland had left the gentlemen to their port, Tony watched young Jack stirring restlessly in his chair. He knew very well he was trying to decide how to broach the information he had been instructed to relay, and Tony magnanimously decided to help him in his task.

"I say, Squire," he said casually, twirling the wine gently in his glass, "I rode about this afternoon inspecting the countryside. Who on earth owns that very ramshackle property on your eastern borders? I have seldom seen such good land in such poor repair!"

"That would be Wardley Hall," the squire replied, sadly shaking his head. "Did you know Robert Ward? He was much in evidence in London before his death; perhaps if he had spent more time at the Hall, things would not now be in such a sad case!"

Tony denied any knowledge of the improvident gentleman as his host continued. "A charming man he was, but careless and reckless to the point of insanity. He ran through a perfectly good inheritance with his gambling and wild schemes, and leaves his family in bad straits, for he died only a month ago. What is to become of them I do not know! There is Melissa, who is Jack's age, then Rob, at seventeen the heir, and a younger sister Nancy, barely thirteen. They are chaperoned by Robert's sister, and if they were left a farthing between them, I have not heard of it. I suspect it will become to selling the Hall. . . ."

"Lissa will never sell Wardley!" Jack broke in impetuously.

"Melissa will have little to say about it, Jack," his father reprimanded him with a frown. "A miss of nineteen! It will be up to the lawyers and any relatives there may be!"

Jack bent his head, and then he asked, as casually as he could, "Did you know they have sold Captain, Father? I guess things are as bad as you say."

"Here, what's this? Sold Captain? And why was I not given first refusal? Melissa knew how much I wanted the horse; Lord, I've told Simon enough times!" The squire seemed indignant at his loss. "Aye, and I would have given them more than he was worth as a way to help them! To think that I've been choused out of owning Captain!" He poured out more wine for Tony, and angrily shook his head. Jack continued manfully, although the squire had evinced no curiosity about the buyer.

"I understand Simon sold him last market day at Washburn . . . to a . . . to a stranger passing through who took a fancy to him."

The squire sniffed. "I shall take Simon and Melissa to task when next I see them. To sell to a stranger when I wanted him!"

The duke broke in easily. "Perhaps the family could not bear to be always seeing their father's horse, as surely they must have had to if you had purchased him. To sell him to a stranger might be thought the least painful way."

Jack flashed him a look of gratitude as the squire nodded thoughtfully. "Perhaps you're right, Tony. That was probably the reason for I know how Melissa loved him! She was forever on his back whenever she could steal him away from her father. A most impressive horsewoman, Melissa Ward! Most impressive!"

"I am sure she must be," the duke could not help murmuring, causing Jack to look at him sharply. As the men rose to rejoin Mrs. Holland in the parlor where she was sitting with her daughters and their governess awaiting the tea tray, he added, "What say you to a ride, young Jack, tomorrow? I've a desire to be taken around the estate!"

Jack looked slightly perturbed, although on past visits he would have been extremely flattered by the proposal. He knew the duke was a top-of-the-trees man and had been warned by his father many times not to make a nuisance of himself by hanging about him like a silly young chub. Now he searched desperately for an excuse as his father threw a burly arm around his shoulders and exclaimed,

"A good idea, Tony! Jack can show you all our latest improvements. I wish I might join you, but there's a matter of business I must attend to."

"I look forward to it," the duke said, giving Jack no time to escape. "I know how busy you are in the morning. Shall we say two o'clock? That will give us time to enjoy one of Mrs. Holland's delicious luncheons!" As this was said just as they entered the parlor, it delighted the lady who broke into protestations about country fare as compared to the delicacies of London that the duke was used to, and gave Jack no time to change the plan. It amused Tony very much to see how distracted the young man was for the remainder of the evening.

CHAPTER 4

The Highwayman Strikes Again

Although Jack thought long and hard for the rest of the evening and through the following morning, he saw no way he could escape the duke's company without appearing excessively rude, and he knew full well his mother and father would never stand for such behavior. So he sent a stable boy to Wardley Hall early, with a carefully worded verbal message to Melissa, warning her of the unexpected company they were to have only to discover that Miss Ward and her aunt had taken Nancy to Washburn that morning and were not expected back till after noon. He tightened his lips and looked so black at this piece of news that the boy made haste to get out of his sight. Jack wished he had Lissa with him now; he'd like very much to shake her until her teeth rattled for getting him involved in this dangerous game!

At two o'clock he had decided to avoid Byway

Brook completely. Too bad if Lissa cooled her heels and thought he had failed! It would do her good! And then later, when the duke had left him, he would ride over to Wardley and try to get a word with her. The duke smiled amiably at him when they met at the stables, and ignored the abstraction that kept Jack from enthusing over the duke's mount, a magnificent gray that he would have been sure to admire at any other time. As they rode from the yard, Jack turned away from the part of the farm where Byway Brook was located and took Tony to see the new drainage system the squire had just had completed in quite another section of the estate. Tony was not surprised. By dint of casual questioning and the study of an old map in the estate room, he had located the brook that very morning, and after he had carefully inspected the new ditches and reclaimed fields, he suggested they make a circuit of the boundaries, and without giving Jack time to propose another plan, wheeled his horse and cantered away. Jack had no choice but to follow him. How it came about he was never quite sure, but at precisely three o'clock he found himself following the duke along the path that ran beside the brook. Tony pulled up when he saw a horse tethered near a grove of trees.

"Why, someone is before us, Jack! Do you know who it might be?"

Jack essayed nonchalance. " 'Tis only Melissa Ward; my father mentioned her last night, you remember. I wonder what she is doing here? Although we are great friends, you know!" he added hastily, as if he felt his explanation had been too offhand. The duke bent down over his bridle to pat his horse and hide a smile, as a girl appeared from behind the trees and called eagerly, "Jack! What happened?" She fell silent as she saw the tall, handsome man accompanying her friend. Jack said nothing as they walked their horses to where she waited, and then, when the duke dismounted and smiled at Melissa, recalled his manners.

"M'lord, this is one of our neighbors, Miss Ward. Melissa, I give you the Duke of Colchester who is visiting my father for a few days."

The duke bowed and examined the latest highwayman as Melissa sketched a curtsey and extended her hand. She was certainly lovely, he thought, even to the critical eye of a connoisseur like himself, and although her habit was shabby and tight, it emphasized her tiny waist and high full breasts. Her color rose as she saw his intent, searching look lingering on her face and then insolently traveling down her figure, making no secret of his approval, and she turned quickly to Jack.

"What a surprise, Jack! I hope you do not mind my trespassing on your property, but it was such a lovely day I rode over to inspect the brook." Her voice sounded stilted, and Jack looked at her in amazement as she reached up a gloved hand to push back an errant curl.

"Why . . . why not at all, Melissa! Well met, I'm sure! And how is everything at Wardley? Rob settled down a bit, has he?"

The duke looked in growing amusement from one to the other. He had not heard such a wooden exchange in many a day; you would have to be a ninnyhammer not to know that something was up! Melissa seemed aware of it for she made an impatient gesture and moved casually away to stand by the brook.

"Things go on much the same. I'll be glad when

Master Rob is back in school!" she said tartly, and then added carelessly, "Of course he is missing my father, and now Captain is gone. You knew we had to sell Captain, Jack? Rob was very fond of him!"

The duke silently applauded this ploy, and then took a hand in the conversation. "It is always sad to sell a good horse, I've found, one that you have been attached to for a number of years, Miss Ward. I have a few old nags I could never bear to let go, such pleasant memories as they provide."

Melissa smiled at him gratefully, and sat down on a boulder as Jack went to tether the horses. "Do you make a long stay, sir?" she asked politely, as the duke stood near her. She wished he would not stare at her in quite such a way. It made her feel breathless when she peeped up at him from under her lashes. He certainly was the picture of a London beau, his beautifully tailored riding clothes perfectly fitting his wide shoulders and powerful legs without a single wrinkle. She was not sure she liked the face under the smart riding hat, although she would not have denied how handsome it was, under the crisp black hair. From the piercing dark eyes and strong nose to the almost sensuous mouth there was something that put her off. Perhaps it was the weary sardonic droop of that mouth and eyelids. He looked a complete devil and no better than he should be. On another occasion she might have been fascinated by him, for she had never met a rake; now she just wished he had not come along and spoiled the meeting. He answered her lightly, "I do not know how long I will be able to remain. I have business in London, and to complete it I am carrying a large sum of money. As soon as I hear from my lawyers I will have to be off."

Melissa watched Jack coming towards them and tried to appear no more than politely interested in this conversational gambit. If she had been a bit wiser and older, she might have wondered why it was necessary for the Duke of Colchester to carry such sums on his person when his credit was good for as much as you liked, and she might also have wondered why he told it to her, a complete stranger. Instead, a little voice in her head said 'The Young Gentleman thanks you for the information, sir!' even as she coolly replied, "I am sure the Hollands will be disappointed if you have to leave too soon, sir."

Jack threw himself down beside her and tried not to scowl at the duke. "I tried to reach you this morning, Lissa, but you were gone to Washburn. I . . . I wanted to ask you to join us on our ride!"

Melissa looked up from where she was dabbling her hand in the water. "Then we are well met, Jack, but indeed, I must not linger. There is always so much to do at the Hall, and I have been gone too long now." She shook the drops from her hand and gave it to him so he could pull her to her feet. The duke lounged back against a tree and watched them silently. Melissa smiled at him as she prepared to leave, and something in the back of her eyes, and the color that came to her cheeks intrigued him. He was sure she had taken the bait!

"Your Grace! It was very nice to meet you and I wish you a pleasant stay and hope you do not have to leave us too abruptly!"

He came forward and walked on her other side towards the horses. "I have just begun to think it would be a great pity if I had to quit the neighborhood *now,* Miss Ward," he said, and why Jack bristled at this innocuous pleasantry was hard to say, for it was uttered with no more than bland politeness, although the teasing glance he gave Melissa might have offended Jack if he had been able to see it.

Melissa smiled again, her blue eyes sparkling up at him, and allowed him to toss her into the saddle. She looked at Jack, her expression pregnant with meaning. "I hope to see you soon again, Jack! My respects to your mother and father!" He nodded and she set Posie in motion.

Both men stood silently watching as she rode away, and when Jack suggested they continue their ride, the duke nodded absently. As they were retracing their route back to Blackwood, he said casually, "I hope I did not interrupt an assignation, my boy!"

Jack flushed indignantly. "No such thing, m'lord! Melissa does not have 'assignations'!"

"The young lady is certainly beautiful enough; I imagine she will have many of them before long, so do not be shy if you are enamored with her. I thought perhaps it was a case with you, and I was an unwelcome third party."

Jack hotly denied that it was any such thing. He had never considered Melissa as anything but a delightful companion and good friend and was completely unaware of her looks. As they rode on, he hoped for some vague reason that the duke's and Lissa's paths did not cross again, although he could not have said why.

Melissa, riding home, was also thinking about the duke. She blushed as she remembered his smile, and the cynical way he had leisurely inspected her. No one had ever dared to look at her like that, as if he were picturing her without her clothes. She glanced down at her habit. It really was tight, she thought in dismay, as she saw how her full breasts pushed against the worn fabric. Perhaps she should reconsider making another, larger one, even though the expense was worrisome. But then, there was small chance that she would see the duke again before he left, for being in mourning made them unable to accept invitations to Blackwood. She wondered why she was sorry this was so. She had not approved of his manner, but she had to admit he was intriguing, and certainly handsome. And then she chuckled to herself. So, he was carrying a large sum of money, was he? She would have to be sure to find out when he was leaving Blackwood!

In the days that followed, Melissa managed to meet Jack alone several times. He was relieved when she made no further plans for midnight rides on Captain, not knowing she was patiently waiting for the duke's departure. She questioned him casually about the duke as she would have about any chance guest at Blackwood, for visitors were an event, and Jack answered her readily. The talk of the latest highwayman died down when he made no further appearances, and outside of daily rides to tend to Captain, Melissa bided her time. She saw the duke only at a distance, and he did not appear to notice her. Well, why should he, she asked herself scornfully, when she admitted she was disappointed by this cavalier treatment. What was she to him but a country miss of no importance? Aunt Cardell was busily remodeling some warm winter gowns for Nancy, and Melissa was glad she had not bothered to ask her aunt to make her a new habit.

And then, one morning in the village, where she had gone in the gig to purchase some supplies for her aunt, she came face to face with the gentleman coming out of the village's only shop which also served as receiving office for the mail.

"Miss Ward, how delightful!" he said in his careless drawl. "Let me help you down." He extended a large hand to assist her from the gig, and Melissa wished she had worn her newer gown, not this old black one that Aunt Cardell insisted on when she went to the village. She was not aware that black complimented her glossy black curls and set off her creamy skin to perfection, the only color her bright blue eyes and blushing cheeks. The duke admired her lazily. She was lushly beautiful and refreshingly unaware of her charms, he thought, and the glimpse of a neatly turned ankle did not escape those keen, dark eyes as she stepped down from the gig.

"Your Grace!" she acknowledged him, feeling a little breathless. "You are still with us? I am sure the Hollands are delighted that you have been able to stay and did not have to ride off to London as you feared."

The duke thought he had seldom met anyone who came more quickly to the point. He bowed slightly. "Unfortunately, Miss Ward, I have just received word that the tiresome business I mentioned to you has become urgent. I fear I must quit Blackwood tonight, after dinner."

Melissa was thinking furiously, and did not question what surely must be thought a singular hour for beginning a journey. Why not wait until morning, a more prudent person would have asked, but since it did not suit her purpose to have him driving away in the bright sunlight, she could only applaud this decision, even as she schooled her features to betray only a mild interest.

"Indeed?" she murmured, "I am sure you travel in

great state, sir, with outriders and guards, do you
not? You must be sure to come by way of the village
and give all the locals a treat!" This last was uttered
in what she hoped was a light, teasing manner.

"No, indeed, I'm not so proud!" the duke retorted,
enjoying himself hugely. "I always travel alone,
with only my coachman. And since I have never
been stopped, it appears that there are such things
as guardian angels, no matter how mortals may
scoff at the idea!"

"May I wish you a pleasant journey, Your Grace?"
Melissa replied, now she had the information she
sought. She gave him her hand and curtsied in
farewell, and then she swept by him into the shop,
her head in a whirl. Tonight! And right after dinner!
Now how was she to manage that? She would have
to think up some story that would account for her
absence from the dinner table if she were to be in
position in time. Of course, the Hollands ate later in
deference to their guest from London, but surely he
would be setting out by nine o'clock, and from the
gates of Blackwood to the copse was only a few
miles. By the time she reached home, although she
could not have told you a single detail of the trip, so
deep in thought as she had been, she had her plans
made. She would tell Aunt Cardell that she wasn't
feeling well—perhaps a touch of stomach trouble as
well as the headache she intended to claim. That
would take care of her nonappearance at the dinner
table. And she would beg to be left alone, completely
alone, so she could try to sleep. Then when Aunt and
Nancy had fussed over her, bringing her lavender-
soaked handkerchiefs for her forehead, and pastilles
to burn, and all the other remedies her aunt swore
by, she would ask them to let her sleep, and not

disturb her till morning. She planned to slip down the stairs while they were eating, leaving her bedroom door firmly shut. There was no guarantee that Aunt would not look in on her before bedtime, but she could arrange her pillows so it would look as if she were lying there in bed to a casual glance. She would have to be very careful to avoid being seen on the roads and lanes while she was riding Captain. No one would think anything of it if they saw her on Posie on a lovely summer evening, but Captain was another story!

She hated to lie to her aunt, and Nancy was so sweet and solicitous that she really did have a slight headache when they finally pulled down the blinds and tiptoed from her room. Aunt Cardell begged her to sleep as long as she liked in the morning, and promised her she would not be disturbed. Melissa arranged the bed carefully, packed her highwayman's breeches, shirt, and vest into a neat bundle, and then she waited impatiently until she heard Aunt Cardell calling Nancy and Rob to dinner. When she was sure they were busy at the table, she made her way quietly to the stable, and was soon on her way, carefully avoiding the side of the Hall where the dining room was located, to avoid being seen.

Captain whinnied to her when she rode into the farmyard, and she soon had him saddled, her clothes changed to breeches and shirt, and the pistols loaded and packed with her coat in the saddlebag. She had brought Mr. Colbert's gold watch, for she did not want to leave the farm too early, but she found the waiting just as hard there as it had been in her room. The minute hand seemed to creep around the dial as she sat on an old barrel and played with the two cats while she waited for the dusk. At eight o'clock she could stand it no longer and mounted Captain and rode from the yard. She tried to go slowly so as to take up more time, but then she saw a gig behind her, and spurred Captain on before the driver could draw nearer and identify them, and once she turned off into a country lane to avoid two riders coming towards her. It was with a sigh of relief that she finally reached her hiding place in the little wood. The late summer evening was deepening with shadows, and the sun was almost down when she dismounted and tied Captain to a tree. Knowing now that she would have plenty of time to prepare, she did not don the heavy coat and only tied the handkerchief loosely around her neck while she checked the pistols. There seemed to be a lot of traffic on the post-road this early in the evening; mostly single riders and an occasional farm cart loaded with hay or produce. She prayed that by the time the duke arrived she would have the road to herself; it would be too bad if her quarry escaped her because there were others in sight! She almost put on her coat and mounted as she heard the sound of coachwheels, but then she realized they were coming from the wrong direction, and she sighed. As she looked at the watch again in the fading light, she saw it was almost nine. She hoped the duke would be relaxed and sleepy after Mrs. Holland's farewell dinner, and therefore more apt to be surprised, as she shrugged on the heavy coat and tightened her mask. When she was back up on Captain she tried to relax and took several deep breaths to steady herself. It must be too early for the owl; she wished she could hear him hoot as a signal that all would go well. For some reason she was more nervous tonight than on her first attempt, although Captain behaved beautifully, and seemed to accept the waiting amongst the dark trees as a normal thing to do.

At last she heard a coach coming from the direction of the village, and grasped her pistol carefully. It was moving at a good clip as it came around the bend, and she recognized the matched team of chestnuts that Jack told her the duke owned. Allowing for the faster pace, she kicked Captain hard and rode full tilt towards the coach, brandishing the pistol. The coachman was alone and pulled up his team obediently as she fired over his head. The coach had come to a halt quite close to her and she quickly had the other pistol aimed at his head.

"Throw down your weapon!" she demanded harshly, and was relieved when he obeyed without question. "Now get down and walk before me!" She had decided to use him as a shield in case the duke carried a pistol within the coach. He tied the reins so the horses wouldn't bolt and did as he was bid, casting nervous glances over his shoulder at her as he scurried to the door of the coach.

"Open it at once! You, in there . . ."

All of a sudden, she was pulled roughly out of the saddle from behind, and as she struggled and Captain tried to rear, the coachman discarded all signs of terror and briskly grabbed the bridle. A large fist held her right arm in a painful twist until she was forced to drop the pistol to the ground, and then the duke's soft drawl came from the interior of the coach.

"Tie his hands before him, and throw him in here, Findle!"

"Aye, Your Grace," her captor muttered, and Melissa almost wept with fear and frustration as she realized that the man must have crept out of the

coach on the other side while she was busy with the
coachman, and come up behind her. Almost as if the
duke knew he was going to be robbed, she thought
wildly, as her hands were bound tightly and she was
pushed up the steps and inside. The duke forced her
to a seat beside him, and ordered his servants to tie
Captain to a leading rein behind the coach and then
proceed. Melissa was glad her mask was still cover-
ing her face, but she had no illusions about the game
being up and was heartsick over her fate.

As they began to move, the duke turned towards
her, his eyes raking what he could see of her face
carefully, and then he gave a small nod and smiled.
Melissa stared back silently.

"Well, and here we have 'The Young Gentleman,'
I'll be bound," he said. "Most foolhardy of you, my
boy, to attempt to hold me up. If Findle had not been
within, I would have been obliged to shoot your head
off. Oh, yes," he added, "a pistol was trained on you
all the time! So unwise to underestimate your opponent! Unfortunately you will not be able to profit
from the lesson, for your highwayman days are now
over . . . permanently!"

Melissa shivered but could not make a sound. If
she begged him, would he perhaps let her go? Maybe
if she told him who she was . . . she turned towards
him and then noticed through the window that the
coach had not turned around and headed back towards Blackwood.

CHAPTER 5

A Dangerous Escape

"Where . . . where are you taking me?" she asked, remembering to use the gruff tone of voice she had adopted as a highwayman. "This ain't the road to Blackwood!"

The duke leaned back at his ease on his side of the carriage. "We are not going to Blackwood," he said calmly.

"But . . . but, I don't understand! I thought you meant to see me hang!"

He smiled briefly before answering. "Did you? But that would be distressingly vindictive of me, would it not? Especially since you did not succeed in robbing me after all."

"But what are you planning to do?" she asked, her heart beating wildly, as she tried to appear indifferent. Her one chance of escaping punishment lay in his taking her back to the squire who would surely help her, horrified with her though he might be! She tested her bonds surreptitiously, but the men had been much too thorough, so there was no help there. She threw the duke a quick glance and was disconcerted to find he was staring at her, a small smile curling his lips. It was a distinctly knowing and unpleasant smile, she thought.

"Do not try to loose the rope, I would hate to have to shoot you or throttle you, my dear Miss Ward," he said softly.

"Miss Ward?" She tried to laugh heartily, but knew it came out as a miserable squeak. "Aye, but you're mistaken, sir! I'm no maid!"

The duke sighed. "Shall we discontinue the playacting? Believe me, it has served its turn!"

Suddenly he grabbed both her hands in one of his own and with his free hand pulled the mask from her face. She gasped as he calmly undid the buttons of her coat. Melissa realized she was very close to hysterics, and took a deep breath to calm herself. The duke smiled, his dark eyes very close to hers. "Ah, what wonders a highwayman's greatcoat can hide!" he said sarcastically, as she blushed scarlet. "You really did not think you could fool me, did you? I have a vast amount of experience behind me, my dear, so much so that I am considered an authority on women! Of course," he added modestly, "overhearing your conversation with young Jack that afternoon in the gazebo was a great help! And," he added grimly, "you should be extremely grateful I did hear it! I always carry a loaded pistol, and if I had not known your identity I would have blown your head off!"

Melissa stared at him helplessly. She had a tremendous desire to burst into tears, but somehow she did not think that would move the duke one little bit; in fact he probably expected her to cry and plead with him. Defiantly, she put up her chin and took another steadying breath, and was horrified when the duke chuckled in appreciation.

"Oh, yes, hanging is much too tame a fate!" he said, dropping her hands and returning to his own side of the carriage while Melissa tried to pull her coat together.

"You may relax, my dear. I have no intention of deciding your fate in a carriage. In a short time we will be at an inn where I have reserved rooms. After supper and a leisurely glass of wine we can determine what happens next." He looked at her white, strained face and smiled. "It is not at all flattering to have you look so frightened! Most women would not be at all unhappy to find themselves alone with me. Let me assure you you will soon feel more the thing!"

"Never!" Melissa exclaimed. "I'd rather hang!"

The duke laughed out loud. "I could give you references, you know. There are several ladies who would vouch for me as being vastly preferable to what you highwaymen call 'the nubbing cheat.' " He paused, courteously waiting for her reply, and when she turned her head away and refused to speak, he added kindly, "I can see that carriages make you fretful, dear Lissa. Now I myself am feeling extremely cheerful and full of conversation; what a great deal we have to learn about each other, to be sure!"

He chuckled as she shuddered, and then added as the coach hit a particularly bumpy stretch of road, and they were both forced to brace themselves with the side straps, "What did I tell you? Even the most luxuriously sprung coach is no place for a serious conversation!"

Stung into speech, Melissa retorted, "I cannot imagine what difference the location makes, Your Grace! Besides, it grows late! You know I must get home as soon as I can!"

"I am afraid it is too late for that," the duke said calmly. "Whether you return home tonight, next week, or a year from now is of small importance. But come, you are too serious! You seem to make me the villain of the piece when, after all, I am considered a gentleman!"

"Only by your title!" Melissa snapped, and then added quickly, afraid of angering him, "If you *are* a gentleman, you will let me go!"

"Let you go? Before we have determined your punishment? Certainly not!" The duke looked stern, although inwardly he was vastly amused. He had given no thought to what he would do with the chit after he caught her at her game, but had firmly determined to teach her a lesson, and one that would deter her from ever taking to the road again.

"Besides, you will not want to leave me, very shortly. Why, I would wager anything you like that I could make you fall in love with me within the year!"

"How much would you wager?" Melissa whispered, fascinated in spite of herself at this solution to her problems.

"Shall we say a thousand guineas? Unless, of course, you consider that paltry?"

She stared at him aghast, knowing that if she lost the bet there was no way she could repay him. He leaned back carelessly, watching her consider the possibilities, and knew she would agree. Her head came up and she thrust out her bound hands. "You have a wager, Your Grace!" she said with quiet dignity. "There is no way on earth that I could possibly fall in love with *you!*"

He threw back his head and laughed out loud. "My ego, alas, my poor ego! I see you will have a salubrious affect on me, Lissa! Any thoughts of my irresistible charm will quickly be banished!" He took her hands and shook them solemnly, but when she glanced at him, she saw that his eyes were twinkling, and his dark face was lit up in that devil's grin.

"I perceive you are a rake, sir! Have I the term correctly?"

"You do indeed, my dear! Gambling, boxing, drinking, wenching . . ." he bowed to her ironically, "I'm your regular rakeshell! Not that that prevents mamas with marriageable daughters from pushing their little darlings at me in droves. Dear, dear! I fear it is my title and my fortune that attracts them!"

"I am sure it must be that," Melissa agreed cordially. "It most certainly cannot be your shyness and good manners, or the polished way you begin an acquaintance!"

The duke laughed again, not at all put out by her frank assessment of his character. "I foresee an enjoyable year! But let me warn you my dear, I play to win! And now, may I suggest you get some rest? It is still some distance to the Running Fox."

He patted her hands, slid his beaver over his eyes, put his head back against the squabs, and appeared to doze off immediately. She noticed he kept his hand on the side pocket where he had placed the pistols, as she buttoned her coat with shaking fingers and tried to think what she could possibly do to escape her dilemma.

Above them, on the box, Findle muttered to the coachman, " 'Ere now, wot's all this? Why head for the post-road? Why not the nearest judge?"

The coachman concentrated on a tricky curve before replying.

"Never question the duke, my man, as you'll find out when you've been in 'is service a bit longer. If 'is lordship says the post-road, the post-road it'll be, toot sweet!" He laughed as the guard clutched the box as they raced through the night. "That's French, Mr. Findle, for go like 'ell!"

Unable to follow the duke's example and sleep, Melissa stared out of the window. The only solution that immediately occurred to her was to throw herself out of the coach, but at the speed they were traveling she would be sure to kill herself! Perhaps if she explained why she was robbing people he might sympathize and let her go—but no, she knew it would be no use. To think that she, Melissa Ward, had come to this! She stole another glance at the duke. With the hat over his eyes, she could see only his arrogant nose and scornful mouth; his chin was sunk in his cravat. She knew the strength of his hands, physically she was no match for him, but she had to escape! And sometime soon a chance would come; she would have to be very watchful for it, and not hesitate, for her escape was all important. She knew there was a double standard for men and women. No one thought it amiss that gentlemen should set up their mistresses both before and after marriage; in fact it was the accepted thing, why, even the Prince Regent she had heard was not immune! But there was also a double standard for women.

There were actresses and opera dancers and servants, and no one cared if they had lovers; marriage was not for them. The quality was different. Their daughters were protected like delicate flowers until they married. They were not allowed to step out of doors without a footman in attendance, and they were chaperoned wherever they went so that in many cases the first time they were alone with a man who was not a relative was when he proposed, after gaining permission to do so, of course. Their most valuable asset was their purity. And she as a Ward was one of their number, not a young maid to be seduced by the master of the house! How could she marry as she planned if she lost her reputation? She did not give the duke credit for silence where women were concerned, and she was sure he would bandy her name the length and breadth of London at the first opportunity! She sighed, and closed her eyes wearily, and without planning to, fell into an uneasy slumber as the coach continued to race onward through the night.

She woke abruptly when it slackened speed somewhat as they reached the outskirts of a town and proceeded at a more decorous pace until they turned into the yard of the Running Fox. Oh, why had she fallen asleep? She had no idea where they were, or how long they had traveled! If she could escape, it would be that much more difficult to get back to Wardley. The town seemed very quiet so it must be late, even though two ostlers appeared promptly to take charge of the coach. The duke was obviously expected. He woke and stretched as Findle opened the door, staring openly at Melissa in amazement. She clutched her coat as the duke ordered her to get down and followed close behind her. He took her arm firmly and ushered her up the shallow steps to the front door, saying over his shoulder, "Stable the horses!" Her heart sank.

She found herself in a small hall where a liveried servant stood bowing and beaming at them.

"There you are, Minton! I see you received my message. Please fetch the small dressing case and bring it to my rooms. Come, my dear. . . ."

He took the candle the servant held out as Minton coughed and said, "Your Grace! I have brought an urgent message from Lord Marshall. Shall I . . . ?"

The duke interrupted as he guided Melissa ruthlessly up the stairs. "I'll hear when I come back!"

Melissa found herself in a large chamber at the front of the inn. She whirled as she was released so he could put the candle down, and moved away from him when she saw the expression on his face, serious and purposeful. He bowed to her.

"I am desolated to have to leave you, Melissa, even for a little while, but I know Lord Marshall and his 'messages!' I shall arrange to have some supper sent up shortly; in the meantime, you might profitably spend the time considering your sins. Dear me! I find myself rather unusually cast in the role of moral mentor! It is certainly a novel experience!" He chuckled at the thought and then came to untie her hands. "Do not do anything foolish! The door, of course, will be locked behind me!"

Melissa found her voice as she rubbed her wrists. "Your Grace! Why do you do this? You know I am a Ward and not a common doxy! I am sure my lineage is as good as your own! I did not think that even members of the Corinthian set would ruin someone, who is, like them, a member of the quality!"

The duke hesitated and turned back to her. "You

lost all right to any consideration of your birth when you embraced the profession of highwayman! You thought me a plum to be plucked and fully intended to rob me if you could. Now the tables are turned, and *you* are the plum! If you would be so bold, you must be prepared to take the consequences! Besides, my dear, if you were 'a common doxy' I would have no interest in you at all!"

Melissa tried again. "Please, Your Grace . . ."

"I give you leave to call me 'Tony,' my dear. 'Your Grace,' sounds so terribly formal between . . . er . . . intimate friends, don't you agree?"

Melissa swallowed the retort that came to her mind and continued calmly. "Very well, Tony, then. You have had your revenge; please let me go! You must realize that my family will be very disturbed by my absence! Perhaps I can reach Wardley before my Aunt Cardell lets the world know that I am missing. . . ."

The duke strolled to her, raising a languid hand on which a great signet ring flashed. "Let you go?" he asked in disbelief, although he was enjoying teasing her. "When I have gone to such pains to get you here? What does it matter if you return now or in a month, let us say? The damage has been done! You cannot reach Wardley tonight, even if you left immediately, and so you have become a very *un*respectable young lady, and your racing back to the home stable will not restore that respectability. Resign yourself! I have not an ounce of philanthropy in my makeup! Perhaps tomorrow you may write your aunt if you wish; I am sure she will be able to fabricate a story about a visit to friends. Besides, I am sure you will feel differently in a very short time—remember our wager!"

He smiled at her confidently, although her white, frightened face almost undid his resolve to continue the farce. Miss Ward would take great care what she did from now on, he thought, as her temper exploded.

"I will never feel any differently about *you!* You can keep me here forever and I will still hate you!"

The duke stepped close to her and grasped her by the shoulders, his quick, easily aroused temper getting the best of him. When Melissa tried to hit him, he imprisoned both her hands behind her back and drew her close. Looking down into her angry, tear-filled eyes and quivering mouth he was unable to resist bending his head and kissing her. His mouth was firm and warm, and Melissa was horrified to find a part of her that she had never known existed wanted to respond to him. He raised his head and smiled at her. "You see, I told you you would feel differently!" Suddenly he released her as a discreet knock sounded at the door, and laughed as she staggered.

"Ah, Minton. Put the dressing case there and come with me!"

The manservant bowed to her as he placed the case on the writing table before withdrawing. She heard the sound of the key in the lock, and then the duke calling for the innkeeper before a door slammed further down the passage. She looked around at her surroundings for the first time. The room had low beamed ceilings and a soft, faded rug. A small fire burned to take off the chill, and before the fireplace was a table covered with a white cloth and settings for two. She shuddered. There were some comfortable chairs and a small sofa, and in one corner, the writing table. For decoration, a row of pewter plates marched across the mantlepiece. There were two small windows covered with chintz curtains, and curiously she went and peered outside. The room faced the inn yard, deserted at the moment. The duke's carriage and Captain must have been taken to the stables. Eagerly she tried to raise the sash, but it had been painted shut so many years that it refused to open. She stood, disconsolate, and then she went to the other window. Although it did not move for a long, heartbreaking moment, she finally succeeded in raising it. Cautiously she put her head out and looked around. Below her was the jutting roof of a bay window. From the lights and noise that issued from it, it had to be the tap room. At the corner of the inn there was an old tree, and one of the branches stretched almost to her window. Perhaps . . . if she got out quietly onto the roof and edged her way to it, she could reach it and swing along it to the trunk. She blessed Jack for making her learn how to climb trees when they were younger. Looking down again, it seemed a very long way to the ground!

Lissa turned back into the room, and seeing the writing table again could not resist leaving the duke a note. She moved the dressing case abruptly, and one of the drawers opened and disclosed a pile of handkerchiefs and a roll of money. Here was the means for her escape, for if she could not find Captain and release him without being seen, she would need the money to get home. But still she hesitated. If she stole it, it would make her as bad as the duke thought she was! Suddenly she remembered Mr. Colbert's watch, and a triumphant smile crossed her face as she dug it out of her greatcoat pocket. She took a sheet of paper and a quill, and after considering for a moment, wrote the duke a few terse sentences.

"Your Grace," she began abruptly,

> Please forgive me if I find myself unable to enjoy any more of your gracious hospitality and distinguished attentions! I know you will understand why I had to make so free with your money. In exchange, I leave you this very fine gold watch, for I have no time to seek a jeweler. Until a year from now when I will collect my wager,
>
> > I am, yours sincerely, etc.
> > The Young Gentleman

She smiled again as she read it over and added a few underlines, and then she put the roll of soft safely away and leaving the note and the watch propped up on the supper table, went hastily to the window. She hesitated a moment, one booted leg over the sill, but there was no sound from below, and drawing a deep breath, she let herself out of the window until her feet rested lightly on the roof of the bay window. Turning to face the wall, she inched along until she could almost touch the branch, and then, praying it would hold her, she let it take her full weight. It creaked ominously, but did not break, so she swung quickly along it till she reached the trunk. In a few moments, she was on the ground, shaken and dirty, with her hands stinging from contact with the rough bark. She crept to the corner and peeked around. The stable was off to one side and as she watched, a pair of ostlers came out and headed for the side door. She waited for a few moments, and then ran to the stable. It was reassuring to hear Captain whinny to her, and she soon had him saddled again, even though her hands were clumsy with nervousness. Such marvelous luck could not last forever! Any moment now, the duke would be rejoining her for supper *à deux* and her absence would be discovered. Surely the first place he would think to look would be the stable! Captain stood quietly for her, and she was soon leading him through the cobblestoned yard to the road, trying hard not to glance behind her. She expected to hear a cry of alarm at any moment, and she shivered. She mounted and turned away from the inn gratefully. She had no idea how to get home, but she felt safer with every yard that separated her from the duke, and did not even think of the dangers she faced, alone at night and far from home.

It seemed a long time before they reached the outskirts of the town and she was able to urge Captain to a canter. He responded a little more slowly than he normally would, and when he stumbled slightly, she knew he was as tired as she was. As soon as she could, she left the highroad and entered some woods that bordered it, following a narrow path until she came to a brook. Dismounting, she tethered Captain to a tree branch. She had hoped to reach home before her absence was discovered, but she knew it was dangerous to travel on strange roads in the dark when they were both so tired. Besides, if the duke rode after her on a fresh horse, as she fully expected him to do, he would be sure to catch them up. She shuddered, imagining his rage! It was much safer to wait until morning when she could leave the main roads and still find her way home. She wrapped her coat around herself more securely and settled down on the hard ground to sleep till dawn. Just as she was dropping off, an owl called, and reassured by the sound that had meant good fortune before, she slept.

She woke, stiff and dirty, to the sound of birdsong, and was dismayed to see that judging by the sun, she had overslept. She brushed herself off as best she could, washing in the cold brook water, and then she remounted and turned again to the post-road, casting many an anxious glance over her shoulder until she reached a small village. The one inn was shabby and poor looking, which exactly suited her present condition, so she rode in and handed Captain over to an ostler to feed and brush down while she strode to the inn for some food and hot coffee. It was fortunate she had the duke's money, and she was soon feeling much better for her breakfast. As she rode away, she was confident she had escaped, for the inkeeper had given her clear directions that would allow her to reach home without traveling the main roads.

CHAPTER 6

Lady Throckmorton to the Rescue

Her spirits rose the closer she got to Wardley, and she began to think she might be able to slip back into the house with no one the wiser. Except Aunt Cardell, she reminded herself. She would have to tell her something and she was pondering what story she might concoct when she saw Jack Holland galloping down the road towards her. His face was white and angry looking and her heart sank, although she raised her hand in greeting and halted Captain. Jack turned his horse and came up beside her, so furious that he didn't even give her a chance to speak.

"Where the devil have you been, Lissa? Your aunt discovered your absence and spoke to Simon; and he suggested she ask me! How do you think I felt, telling them you had gone for a highwayman?"

"Oh, Jack, you didn't!" Melissa wailed.

"Of course I did, you little idiot! How else could I

83

explain it except by the truth when you might have been lying somewhere wounded and bleeding to death?"

"Does anyone else know?" Melissa asked, a pleading look in her eyes as she studied her friend's angry face.

"No, I don't think so," he replied more calmly as the horses moved forward again at a walk. "Your aunt told the household you were sick and couldn't be visited since she feared it might be contagious!"

"Oh, clever Aunt Cardell! Now, all I have to do is get back into my room with no one seeing me, and all will be well!"

"It will not be well!" Jack exploded again. "Where have you been all this time? When I think how we have all worried, and your poor aunt beside herself, I could whip you!"

Melissa bowed her head as the tirade swept over her. "Indeed, dear Jack, I am sorry! But . . . but I had to wait such a long time last night for a coach, and then when one finally appeared and I held it up, another horseman arrived and I had to ride away to avoid capture. . . ."

"But it is so late, Lissa! Where have you been all night?"

She could see from Jack's face that he was not to be fobbed off as easily as she had thought, so she drew a deep breath and continued. "I was so frightened, Jack! I had to ride a long way to lose him, and I doubled back and took some strange roads, and finally when I thought I was safe, I didn't know where I was! And Captain was so tired! I thought it best to . . . to hide till morning, so I found a deserted wood and . . . and fell asleep! When I woke up I didn't know the way home and didn't dare to ask anyone! I took several wrong turns before I reached the post-road again." She paused and peeped at him from under her hat. His face was not encouraging.

"I never heard such a tale! Melissa Ward of Wardley sleeping in a wood! And losing your way! It serves you right, you little fool, for such a mad escapade! There'll be no more highwayman tricks for you!"

Melissa sighed in relief that he had accepted her story. "I know, it really is too dangerous as I discovered last night!"

They reached the lane that led to the farm, and she was thankful the way was too narrow for them to ride abreast any longer, but her relief was short-lived for they soon reached the farmyard and the stern face of Simon, shaking his head and exclaiming over her. She repeated her tale while he took charge of Captain and she saddled Posie, and he promised to care for the gelding until she could decide what to do with him. Jack rode with her as far as the lane that led to the Wardley stables, and promised to call on her shortly, to "hear the whole story." Melissa shuddered. No one was going to hear that!

She soon had Posie in her stall and went up to the side door of the Hall and softly let herself in. There were voices at the back of the house, so she slipped quietly up the stairs to her own room. As she closed the door softly behind her, she heard her aunt's voice and turned quickly.

"Thank God you are back, Lissa!" Aunt Cardell exclaimed, rising from a chair by the window and staring at her niece. If she had ever doubted the tale of Melissa Ward turned highwayman, she could do so no longer, not with the evidence before her! Melissa stood there in her breeches and boots, her hair bundled under her hat, and her face smudged with dirt. She looked exhausted and shaken, and Aunt Cardell moved quickly to put her arms around her and hold her close. At that, all Melissa's self-control went, and the careful tale she had told Jack and Simon was forgotten as she poured out the truth with tears streaming down her face. She knew her aunt would be shocked and horrified but it didn't seem to matter. The only part of the story she left out was the duke's kiss and the wager they had made. Aunt Cardell held her tightly and patted her back and said not a word until Melissa told her how she had managed to escape the duke, and then she took her firmly by the hand and led her to the bed.

"Now, Lissa, it is very bad, but you are safe now! What did you tell Jack Holland and the groom?"

Melissa assured her aunt that they did not know what had really happened, much to her aunt's relief, and she became more brisk.

"Do get out of those terrible clothes, girl, and wash while I bring you something to eat! And then you are going to sleep! I do not want you to think about it anymore today!"

Aunt Cardell pushed her firmly towards the washbasin and pitcher, and bustled out of the room. Melissa's eyes widened. She had never expected her confession of highwayman and subsequent capture by the duke to be taken so calmly by her aunt, but here she did Mrs. Cardell an injustice. Shocked she certainly was, but she was so relieved to have Melissa back safely with no one the wiser that it overshadowed any moral considerations that might otherwise have upset her. She had spent the time Melissa was away imagining all the grim possibilities that might be-fall her niece, and so she had heard the story with a profound sense of relief that things were not a great deal worse!

When she returned, Melissa was fast asleep, looking very young and innocent in her white nightgown and clean scrubbed face. She tiptoed away with the tray; sleep was more important now! She came back after dinner to find Melissa stirring. Closing the door carefully, she set her tray down on a table near the bed, then she lit another candle and shook her niece gently. Melissa woke with a start and clutched the sheets until she remembered she was safe at home. Her color rose as her aunt smiled at her, and she turned her head away in confusion.

"Now, my dear," Aunt Cardell said briskly. "You must not be so upset! The duke is an evil man no doubt, but believe me, no one will know anything about your escapade but you and I. *He* will not tell a tale that so discredits him, you may be sure! So, Lissa," she took the girl's chin and made her look at her, "your reputation is safe! There now, sit up and try to eat. You must be hungry."

"Oh, I am starving, Aunt!" Melissa exclaimed, feeling much better for her aunt's matter of fact attitude, and she had to laugh when she saw the invalid fare prepared for her. "What I would really like is my dinner, not this gruel and custard!"

"That is small punishment to pay, miss, for your behavior! I told everyone I thought you were coming down with something contagious, to keep them away from your room. Nancy was hard to restrain, but she made the custard for you with her own hands, so you will eat it cheerfully, if you please! Maybe by tomorrow you can have a miraculous recovery and we will all be relieved that my diagnosis was wrong!"

Melissa put out her hand to her aunt. "Before I

eat, I must tell you how sorry I am to have worried you so, Aunt! It was too bad of me!"

She hung her head as Aunt Cardell hugged her and told her never to mind that now, but to eat her gruel and custard. When she was finished her aunt insisted she sleep again. "I will be up first thing in the morning, my dear, for we must talk seriously about your . . . your adventure. You do see that there can be no repetition of it, I am sure!" Melissa agreed, and dozed off as Aunt Cardell left the room.

The next morning she was dressed and pacing her bedroom floor when her aunt let herself in with some breakfast. As she ate, the older woman questioned her in more detail, and Melissa showed her the gold guineas and jewelry she had taken from Mr. Colbert, and the roll of money she had from the duke. Aunt Cardell was really shocked now; she had had no idea of Melissa's earlier attempt, but she made no mention of that as she blurted out, "But . . . but Lissa! To steal his money after what happened! Not that he didn't deserve it, but . . . but it puts a whole new complexion on things!" Melissa stared at her, bewildered. "I mean," her aunt continued, "it makes you a common thief!" Melissa's cheeks flushed crimson, but she held herself steady.

"No such thing, Aunt! I left him a note and Mr. Colbert's watch in trade!" She did not mention her wager with the duke; she had no intention of ever mentioning that!

Aunt Cardell shook her head sadly. "But Lissa, that watch was not yours to give! You had stolen it! Oh, dear, this is so confusing! Now how can we return the money and the jewelry to Mr. Colbert if you have disposed of his watch!"

Melissa impulsively took her aunt's hand. "Dear

Aunt! We cannot without the whole story coming out. Surely I have been punished enough? And I am most truly sorry!" The tears came to her eyes and she bit her lip before continuing. "I know that stealing is wrong—indeed, I do not know what caused me to take such a criminal step except I was desperate! I had to save Wardley!" She explained her plans for going to London with the proceeds and her aunt stared at her as if she had never really understood her before. At length she rose, shaking her head.

"Well, Lissa, you may come down to luncheon. There is no way we can make this right, I see clearly. It was folly of you to take Wardley as a personal burden. That was for Mr. Bentley and myself, and Rob too, as soon as he is old enough." Melissa stared at her aunt who seemed to grow in dignity as she spoke. "Furthermore, you must promise never to do anything so foolish again!"

Melissa promised, but in the back of her mind the question remained, what would happen to Wardley now?

She made a good lunch, in fact her aunt frowned when the invalid took a second helping of the cheese souffle. Nancy was delighted with her recovery, and Rob contributed some items of gossip he had heard in the village. Melissa smiled at them all. It felt so wonderfully safe to be home!

As they were leaving the table and she prepared to help Prims with the clearing, a knock was heard at the front door. She hoped it wasn't Jack, come to collect his "details," as Prims left slowly to answer the summons. A moment later he returned and said to Mrs. Cardell, "A Lady Throckmorton, ma'am. I have put her in the drawing room."

Aunt Cardell put down the glass she was holding

and looked confused. Melissa smoothed her dress expectantly and even Rob looked interested. "It is Aunt Alice! Hurry, Aunt, take off that apron! I wonder what she wants?"

The lady looked flustered as she patted her hair under the plain cap she wore and removed her apron. "Do you come with me, Lissa! Whatever shall I say? Oh, why did I wear this old gown today? I look a complete drab! What is she like, Prims?"

The old butler sniffed. "Very fashionable, I would say, ma'am, and looks much like the late Mrs. Ward."

Melissa whispered to Nancy, "Do help Prims with these dishes, will you, love? And don't go far! I want you to meet our new aunt too!" She shepherded Aunt Cardell to the hall before that lady could decide she must change her dress, and then they both stood speechless in the drawing room, staring at the vision before them.

Lady Throckmorton was a tiny blonde, dressed in palest blue. Her bonnet was adorned with feathers and ribbons and perfectly matched her gown, as did her light mantua, lined with swansdown, which she held over one gloved arm. She smiled sweetly at them, and looked so girlish that Melissa exclaimed, "Oh, there must be some mistake! You cannot be our aunt, ma'am! You are much too young!"

The lady's smile broadened as she swept towards them, both hands extended. "Dear girl! How can you say so? Althought I *was* a great deal younger than my sister Anne!" She embraced Melissa fervently, and Melissa was able to see that close up, her aunt was nowhere near as young as she had first appeared. She was painted and powdered with great care, but the lines still showed.

"And who might you be? Surely you are too old to be my niece?" she asked gaily, a small frown between her eyes as she studied Melissa's dark curls and lovely face.

Melissa curtsied. "I am Melissa Ward, the oldest, m'lady, and this is my aunt, Mrs. Cardell."

Lady Throckmorton gave her hand graciously to Aunt Cardell. "So pleased! I must introduce my husband. Where have you got to, Ferdie?" A very tall, very thin gentleman rose from the wing chair near the fire where they had not noticed him before, and approaching, bowed to them both.

Aunt Cardell remembered her manners. "Won't you be seated, m'lady, m'lord? May I send for some refreshments, or perhaps you have not had luncheon?"

Lady Throckmorton took a seat, still holding Melissa's hand and studying her. "A glass of wine would be lovely. We have been traveling since dawn, but we did stop for refreshments on the post-road."

Lord Throckmorton spoke for the first time. "M . . . M . . . Must protest, m'dear! Must protest! Left London at eleven, not a moment before, p . . . p . . . pon my word!" He looked gloomy and then added, "You decided not to wear pink!"

Lady Throckmorton's laugh pealed out. "I am *always* late! Poor Ferdie, I am the bane of his life, for with the best of intentions I cannot come up to scratch on time!" Melissa could not help smiling at her and the lady clapped her hands. "Why, you are the spit of Robert when you smile! Do you not see the likeness, Ferdie? Are the other children like their father, or do they favor my sister?"

Melissa noted that her voice hardened a bit when she spoke of her sister, and the warmth left it, but she replied easily, "We are very like, all three of us. May I ask my brother and sister to join us, ma'am? They would so like to meet you too!"

"And I am dying to see them! Dear little Rob, and the little girl too! I wish we might have been with you before this, my dear," she added, "but Ferdie and I have been traveling abroad, and your letter was not forwarded to us. What a sad thing for you all; dear Robert dead! I still cannot believe it!" She wiped her eyes with a lace handkerchief as Aunt Cardell left the room to fetch the children and make sure that Prims brought the good glasses and the wine on a presentable tray. Lady Throckmorton continued.

"Forgive me if it gives you pain, Melissa, but I do not think things have gone very well with you since your father's death—or even before! Anyone can see how badly the estate is run down, and the drive! So overgrown I expected a witch to pop out and cast a spell over us! And this room! So . . . so shabby!"

Lord Throckmorton straightened up from where he had been leaning against the mantle and protested. "I say, m'dear! Easily over the ground, I beg of you!"

"Pooh!" Lady Throckmorton exclaimed, ignoring Melissa's blush. "I am their aunt, and I can say what I like! There is no hiding poverty that is shown so plain!"

Before Melissa could reply, Nancy and Rob came in, and she was proud of them both. Nancy curtsied very nicely, her big eyes wide and curious, and Rob was very much the young gentleman. Aunt Alice went down on her knees and hugged Nancy to her. "Oh, my dear! How very pretty you are! And Rob! So handsome, and so much like your dear father!" Her eyes misted slightly again and the lace handkerchief again came into play. Rob bowed, his color heightened until Lord Throckmorton took pity on him and asked a question about his school. Soon he was conversing easily, and Nancy was shyly answering her aunt's questions about her pony and her friends.

When the wine had been served and Prims had bowed his way out and closed the door, Lady Throckmorton looked to her husband and said, "I do think we should, don't you, Ferdie? Dear Robert's children!" Ferdie nodded, but before he could speak she hurried on. "I have no head for business, as Ferdie can tell you my dears, but it appears that you need our assistance in the worst way! How were things left? What money is there? Please be frank; we are your closest relatives, you know!"

Aunt Cardell cleared her throat and spoke with dignity. "After me that is so, ma'am. The estate has been left in trust for Rob until he comes of age, and the lawyer Mr. Bentley and I have been named executors. If you were acquainted with my brother you would know there is not a great deal of money, but we shall manage."

She looked very much the grand lady as she spoke, but Lady Throckmorton laughed gaily. "Now do not be offended, my dear Mrs. Cardell, I beg of you! Ferdie can tell you I have no tact, no tact at all, and just rush in for that is my nature!" She waved her little hands and Melissa admired the jewels displayed as she continued. "Indeed I knew poor Robert! I gather he has left you all very poorly off. You must allow us to come to your rescue for Ferdie is fabulously wealthy! I cannot begin to spend all his money!"

"M'dear!" the long suffering peer objected. "It's not for want of trying!"

Lady Throckmorton ignored this sally. "And we

have no children of our own. Surely you would not be so proud as to deny us this treat? Why, I insist!"

Aunt Cardell would have spoken, but the lady rushed on. "Now children, and you too Melissa! I must ask you to leave us for a short time while your aunt and I come to grips with this problem. Run along now! We will see you shortly!"

In a daze, the three Wards rose and took their leave. In the hall, after Melissa had firmly shut the door on Nancy's curiosity, she turned to find Rob grinning at her, his eyes blazing with excitement.

"There now, Lissa! Our fortunes are made! I knew it would all come right in the end! And you, with your economizing and penny-pinching!"

Melissa smiled back, but she was feeling very uncertain. "I don't know, Rob, whether we should let them help us. Surely it is to humble ourselves, for Lord Throckmorton is not even a blood relation."

"It is Aunt Alice who runs that family, it's plain to see, and she is Mother's sister," Rob replied.

"But what of the quarrel? We have never seen her till this day!"

"The quarrel was years ago, and who needs to drag up all that ancient history?" Rob asked hotly. "Don't you stand in the way, Lissa, I warn you! I mean to take everything they give!"

Melissa frowned at him as he left them, but she was still bemused by the managing ways of her newest aunt and was soon too busy trying to answer all Nancy's questions to give him much thought.

The two aunts and Lord Throckmorton were closeted in the drawing room for what seemed a very long time, and Melissa was glad when the summons came to rejoin them. Her eyes flew to Aunt Cardell as she entered the room, and she was glad to see that

that lady looked composed although she seemed paler than usual. Lady Throckmorton was drawing on her gloves, and Melissa was surprised at this sign of imminent departure.

"We must rush, yes, positively we must just dash off and leave Mrs. Cardell to explain! A tiresome engagement in town, my dears. Now let me know what you decide, for I shall be on pins and needles until I hear from you!" She hugged Nancy and kissed Melissa lightly when the girl bent her head so she could reach her cheek. "You are tall, aren't you, my dear? And quite tiresomely lovely! Well, I daresay I will grow accustomed! Dear Rob!" She surged forward and kissed him too saying, "The resemblance is so striking! I swear I am quite overcome!"

All during this scene, Lord Throckmorton was taking solemn leave of Aunt Cardell and the Wards in his own quiet way. He looked as bewildered as she felt, Melissa thought as she escorted them to their carriage. Rob's eyes were glowing. Now that was something like, he thought! It was pale blue, the wheels and decorations picked out with gold. A chariot for a princess, Melissa thought in amusement, wondering if she would ever have dared to hold it up! Lady Throckmorton was handed tenderly into this equipage, Lord Throckmorton followed, and the matched team of grays swept them off. The Wards stood on the steps watching the carriage disappear, and then Rob demanded, "Well, what did they say, Aunt? Do not keep us in suspense!"

"Come into the library, all of you," Mrs. Cardell said sternly, and led the way in silence. When they were all seated, she continued.

"It appears that Lord and Lady Throckmorton are desirous of adopting you all; oh, not legally, but

seeing to your welfare. I could not like it, but I don't
deny it would solve all our problems! We have decided that Rob will continue at school. Lord Throckmorton will undertake an allowance for you, Rob,
and they have asked you to visit during holidays.
Nancy will stay at Wardley for the present. I convinced Lady Throckmorton that would be best, for
she rackets about a great deal, and that is not good
for a child. She will be sending you some boxes, my
love; I only hope the clothes she chooses will not be
too unsuitable! As for Lissa, she is to join the
Throckmortons in London as soon as possible. The
lady was very definite about that! She seems to feel
it will take weeks to make you presentable, Lissa!"
Aunt Cardell sniffed contemptuously as Rob gave a
cheer. "Hush, Rob! Of course it is entirely up to you,
Lissa, but I will speak to you about it later."

Melissa opened her mouth to speak, but thought
better of it as Rob and Nancy exclaimed and
questioned. At last she was alone with her aunt, Rob
magnanimously offering to escort Nancy to Blackwood
so she could relay the good news without delay.

"Did you suggest I join them in London, Aunt?"
Melissa asked slowly. "Somehow I cannot feel that
Aunt Alice is overjoyed to be saddled with a grown
girl!"

Her aunt laughed. "No, she does not welcome
competition, especially someone as young and pretty
as you are! Actually, it was Lord Throckmorton who
suggested it. He pointed out the impossibility of
finding you a husband if you remain at Wardley
Hall, and said he was sure your aunt would be
delighted to present you to society. She pouted a bit,
and tried a few excuses. For example, she was sure

you were needed here to help with the estate, but I reassured her!"

Melissa hugged her grim aunt. "And so I am needed! How will you manage without me?"

"There will be no problem there. Lord Throckmorton has offered to send me a good footman and another maid, and he mentioned something about an estate agent and repairs—well, I was so confused at that point I referred him to Mr. Bentley! He promised to see him without delay."

Melissa paced up and down the room, lost in thought. Here was the solution to all her problems, and if she had just waited it would all have come to her without her stealing and being caught by the duke! But how could she play the part of innocence when surely she would have to see the duke in London! Would he publish her adventures to the world? She turned to her aunt confused, and told her her concerns. Mrs. Cardell begged her not to be so silly. "The duke has behaved in a very scaly fashion, Lissa. He will not be at all anxious to publish his behavior abroad, especially since you bested him! If you remain unapproachable and stay well away from him, he will have to follow your lead. You have the protection of Lord Throckmorton after all! As for your 'reputation,' well! You were never a simpering miss and there is no need to become one now. Remember you are a Ward!"

Melissa was not hard to persuade and even ventured a guess that the duke was not acquainted with the Throckmortons; London must be such a very large place! She wrote to accept the invitation that evening although she still had her doubts that her company would be tolerable to a lady who seemed determined to remain young at all costs. How would she explain a niece of nineteen? Lissa thought Lord Throckmorton kind, but she did not depend on his intervention if there were problems; like Rob, she thought it was Aunt Alice who ruled that household! Finally she shrugged. If it didn't work out she could always return to Wardley, and to have her chance in London she was willing to put up with a great deal.

The days until her departure flew by and at last the final morning came. Lord Throckmorton had kindly offered to send his coach for Melissa, and at the same time deliver the servants he had promised Aunt Cardell. Melissa had gone to see Jack and say good-bye. He was pleased for her, and more than slightly relieved that her removal to London would prevent any more highwayman excursions, although he knew he would miss her. She spent a long time in the stables with Simon, making arrangements for Captain's care. She hoped to be able to send for him eventually, and Simon promised to see to it as soon as she wrote.

As Melissa stood on the steps while her trunk was stowed in the boot and the two servants were welcomed by Aunt Cardell, she was overcome with emotion. Wardley looked so beautiful in the late summer light; how she would miss it! And Nancy too, she thought fondly, looking down at her holding tight to her big sister's hand with tears in her eyes which she tried hard not to shed. Even Aunt Cardell was gruffer than usual. At last all was ready, and Melissa hugged Rob and Nancy and promised to write often, and then she kissed her aunt fervently and squeezed her hand in silence, for she knew she could not speak past the lump in her throat.

"Be off with you now, Lissa!" her aunt said, giving

her a little push. "Let us know when you are settled, we will look for your letters!"

Melissa allowed the groom to help her into the luxurious coach and waved to her family on the steps as it tooled away, down the overgrown drive and through the village to the post-road and ... London! She had some hours to think on the journey. How different this was from her last trip when she had been so frightened and humiliated! She wondered where the duke was now; she had half expected him to follow her to Wardley and had lived in terror for some days until she realized he had no such intentions. It annoyed her for some reason that he could be so nonchalant about her disappearance; not, she told herself hastily, that she ever wanted to see him again except to collect her wager! But it was annoying to have him creep into her mind at odd times of the day when it was obvious that he hadn't given her a moment's thought since she had managed to escape.

In this she wronged the duke. He had been coldly furious when he returned to his room and found her gone with the window wide open and the route of her escape plain. He had picked up her note with a frown, but when he read it and saw Mr. Colbert's watch he had to smile. An enterprising young lady, Miss Melissa Ward! His first impulse was to gallop after her, but her escape solved the problem of returning her to Wardley himself, when she had been sufficiently chastened. He was sure he had frightened her enough so that she would never again take to the highroad in her mask and breeches. He admired her bravery, setting out for home in the middle of the night, and was surprised to discover that he hoped she would reach Wardley safely. Eventually he shrugged, and put her out of his mind until he should return to Blackwood and her vicinity. There would be other occasions in the coming year to make sure he won the wager, for no matter how clever the ingenuous Miss Ward might be, he had no intention of being bested by her. He had never been refused by any lady and could not even foresee the possibility of it happening now. He ate his supper alone, stayed the night at the Running Fox, and continued to London the following morning.

Now Melissa sat in her aunt's coach and smoothed her gloves nervously. She looked down at the gray traveling dress Aunt Cardell had worked so hard to get ready. Somehow she did not think Aunt Alice would consider it anything above common. She had the duke's money and the gold guineas she had stolen, for Aunt Cardell had insisted she take them with her. "You must have some money of your own, my love, and although I can never approve of the way it was acquired, you might as well put it to good use. I wish I might give you some of the housekeeping money; alas, 'tis not possible, so be very careful how you spend what you have!"

Melissa had packed the money carefully in her dressing case along with her mother's pearls and a small diamond brooch that had somehow escaped her father's notice when he was selling the jewelry, and hoped she had enough to buy some London gowns. At last the coach slowed as they entered the city. It was so crowded and noisy with people that she was sure the team would run over some of the urchins who darted near the coach. They passed a town crier and on the next corner a vendor crying "Chairs to mend!" He had lusty competition from a farmer in an old cart calling "Milk O! Milk below!" The noise seemed deafening, she hoped she would be able to sleep, and the smells that rose from the open drains and running sewers made her wish she had soaked her handkerchief with lavender water before she left home. At length they drew away from the poorer sections of town, and began to pass intriguing shops and silk warehouses, and then a park and some imposing mansions. She stared at the magnificent facades and porticoes, such a sharp contrast to the crowded tenements and narrow, odor-filled streets and alleys they had just passed.

At last the coach pulled up before the Throckmorton town house. The guard let down the steps and helped her to alight as she clutched her reticule and dressing case and looked about her in wonder. Surely her aunt and uncle lived in one of the most grandiose and elaborate of all! The front door was thrown open, and an imposing butler bowed and welcomed her before sending two liveried footmen to fetch her trunk. She put up her chin, determined not to show any awe or fright. She was a Ward, and somehow she would make this opportunity work for her, Aunt Alice or no!

CHAPTER 7

Miss Ward in London

In no time at all, Melissa was swept up into town life. Aunt Alice was surprisingly kind, as if having committed herself to sponsoring her niece removed all her former objections although she lost no opportunity to mention all she was doing for "dear Robert's child." She would sigh and look so noble that Melissa had trouble restraining a sharp reply and looking suitably grateful. She learned quickly that things went more smoothly if Aunt Alice was unopposed. That lady considered herself the gentlest of creatures and very easy to please, and so she was if no one contradicted her, and everyone fell in with all her plans. She expected instant obedience to her wishes, and liked to think there was never a better mistress, if only servants were not so bent on displeasing her! Why, only last week she had had to let go a very superior dresser when the woman dared to suggest she was wearing too many jewels. And the carelessness of that stupid upstairs maid! Imagine spilling her morning chocolate all over her new lace peignoir and then having the impertinence to claim that Lady Throckmorton had jostled her arm. It was too bad! Ferdie arranged for new servants without a word.

As she suspected, her aunt took one look at her new gray gown and shuddered. "Oh, dear, how dowdy!" she cried with utter unconcern for Melissa's feelings. "Does the woman have no taste? I can see we have a vast amount of shopping to do, dear Melissa! We shall begin in the morning!"

Melissa tried to point out that she did not have much money, but her aunt waved her little hands and declared she was not to consider that for Ferdie would take care of all her bills. When Melissa insisted that she had no intention of becoming a charge on her uncle, her aunt was so much displeased that she dismissed her coldly, saying she was afraid dear Melissa had given her a headache, and she must rest. She remained in her room until dinner time when she was very petulant and chilly to both Melissa and her husband. She insisted the veal scallops were tough, the turbot overcooked, and the jellies inedible. It was a most uncomfortable dinner, and Melissa hastened to speak to her uncle. He begged her to let Lady Throckmorton do as she wished, "for, my dear," he said with a twinkle, "things will go much more smoothly then! Dear Alice cannot abide arguments! They always bring on one of her sick headaches. Assure you, my pleasure to buy you some pretty gowns! And it will give Alice so much delight for she dearly loves to shop!" Melissa agreed reluctantly, and peace was restored.

She was taken on a whirlwind tour of all the best

shops, and had soon lost count of the beautiful clothes
her aunt insisted she needed. There were ball gowns
and day dresses, habits and driving outfits, mantuas
and shawls and spencers and fichus, as well as
bonnets and kid slippers and reticules and gloves,
and all the lacy handmade underthings to go with
them. Lady Throckmorton never asked the price, so
Melissa was completely in the dark as to how much
this was all costing, but she was sure, from the
distinguished attentions they received from mesdames
Thérèse, Fifi and Minette, that it was considerable.
She had never in her life imagined having the kind
of wealth that allowed you to buy anything you
wished, any time you wanted, and sometimes couldn't
help but consider how much better spent the money
would have been in repairing Wardley. Not that she
didn't love her new clothes; they were so beautiful!

There had been another scene when she mentioned
her mourning and the necessity of remaining in
black gloves for a full year. Aunt Alice continued to
hold out the pink muslin she had chosen and stamped
her little foot impatiently. "I absolutely forbid mourning! Too depressing and tiresome for someone with
my sensibilities! It will curtail all my—I mean, *your*
activities and quite defeat our purpose. Besides,
dear Robert would never have wished it! Do try not
to be so stupidly plaguey, my dear!"

Melissa reluctantly agreed, for remembering her
merry, fun-loving parent, she was sure he would
have approved completely of such sentiments.

Lady Throckmorton purchased almost as much for
herself as she did for Melissa. She had only to see a
new gown or a piece of silk she fancied before she
was ordering it made up. Melissa thought some of
her choices more suitable for a younger lady, but she

was learning to keep her tongue between her teeth where her frivolous aunt was concerned. If the lady wished to look like mutton dressed as lamb, as the popular saying had it, it was not for her to point out the error.

Lady Throckmorton also summoned the most popular hairdresser in London to come to the house and cut Melissa's black curls in a more fashionable style. Melissa was astounded when he enthused over them, and Aunt Alice soon had a petulant pout as he continued to admire such natural, luxuriant beauty, until Melissa caught sight of her aunt's face and cut his compliments short.

"But not to compare with Lady Throckmorton's!" she said hastily. "How I have always longed for golden hair! What a shame that you must ever cover it with a bonnet, Aunt, it is so beautiful! I am sure that black is common compared to gold!"

Lady Throckmorton preened and smiled, her good humor restored, and the hairdresser, remembering what a good customer she was and how profitable it was to him to keep the lady's hair that precise golden shade, hastened to agree that black curls paled in comparison.

The first evening Melissa wore one of her new gowns to dinner, she felt almost shy. It was a simple jonquil silk, and because it had been made for her, fit her admirably. Lord Throckmorton was fulsome in his compliments, and turning to his wife said, "Well done, my love! Only you with your exquisite taste could have turned our country mouse into such a stylish young lady!" Lady Throckmorton disclaimed although Melissa could see she was pleased with the compliment.

She had allowed her aunt complete say in what

she wore, with the exception of a black habit she saw and fell in love with. She could not restrain the wish that she might have it, and fortunately her aunt agreed. "Yes, my love, 'twill be ravishing with your black curls and creamy complexion!" Melissa found herself thinking of the duke as the habit was being fitted, and wondering if he would agree.

She expected to see him every time they went out, either shopping or to an evening party, and in the theater spent quite a lot of time searching the various boxes and the floor of the house in dread and anticipation, but so far there was no sign of him. She had no way of knowing that he was visiting friends in Scotland and hunting stags, and although she thought London crowded with the quality, her aunt declared it thin of company for there were several months to go before the season properly opened. The autumn passed quickly, with one amusement after the other, and the days were crowded with the dancing lessons her aunt insisted she have, and the inevitable shopping trips. Melissa saw Vauxhall and was delighted with this famous pleasure place, but what she enjoyed most were her canters in the park with her uncle while Aunt Alice rested for whatever party had been planned for the evening. She was becoming very fond of Lord Throckmorton although she had to stifle a giggle when he begged her to call him "Uncle Ferdie." She discovered he was nowhere near as silly and irrelevant as she had thought; once he was away from his wife he could talk knowledgeably about any number of subjects. One afternoon he alluded to the quarrel between Anne Ward and his wife, and said it was too bad that both ladies had allowed it to cause such a rift. Melissa was anxious to ask more about it, but she did not dare. Lord

Throckmorton seemed to think she knew all the details, and of course it was impossible to ask Aunt Alice! Unpleasant subjects always made her pettish.

She told her uncle about Captain, and he insisted she send for the horse, patting her hand when she tried to express her gratitude for his kindness.

"Come, my dear, leave off! I cannot tell you how delighted I am to do it, for you give us such pleasure! You have become the daughter we never had!"

Impulsively, Melissa hugged him, tears of thanks coming to her eyes, and her uncle colored up and began to stammer. It was not too many more days before Melissa was riding Captain in Hyde Park down Rotten Row, knowing her mount was the equal of any of the horses they saw.

Aunt Cardell wrote regularly and gave her all the news of Wardley which Melissa read eagerly for she could not restrain an occasional pang of homesickness. She learned that Rob had returned to school although he expected to be invited to the Throckmortons' for the Christmas holiday, and Nancy had grown and seemed much happier now, and was quite thrilled with her new clothes, especially a soft velvet cloak with a fur collar! Melissa wondered what they would make of her new gowns, and she tried to be faithful in her letterwriting so they would know all she did. She did not ask her uncle for a frank; it was about the only money of her own she spent outside of a few vails for the servants. She did not mention to her family how confined she felt in London; she could not ride or walk alone as she was used to do at home, and either a groom or a footman was in constant attendance. She sometimes smiled to herself as she remembered holding up Mr. Colbert's coach so boldly, the same Melissa Ward who was now being treated like a very young, very fragile miss.

One evening in November, the Throckmortons were invited to attend a small dance given by Lord and Lady Woodson, and Aunt Alice was especially insistent that Melissa look her very best, even sending her own hairdresser to her after he had finished dressing her own golden hair in an elaborate style. She had chosen Melissa's gown carefully, a simple white gauze over a silver satin slip with matching silver slippers and a ribbon to thread through her curls. When she came to inspect her niece, Melissa exclaimed, for surely Aunt Alice looked very grand this evening! She wore a vivid green satin gown and more flashing emeralds than Lissa had ever seen on one person before, and Melissa felt like a pale ghost beside her. Lady Throckmorton preened before the pier glass.

"Oh, la, my dear, never say so! Of course a married lady is allowed to wear more brilliant colors, but I am pleased with you, Melissa, very pleased. You look just as you ought for a debutante, and reflect well on my taste and discernment. I am sure you will take the shine from all the other girls; in fact I am sure Lady Woodson will pale with envy at my niece. Her daughter is so plain, poor thing!"

This ungenerous thought seemed to afford Aunt Alice a great deal of satisfaction and she smiled happily as she escorted Melissa down the broad stairs to where Ferdie was waiting. He complimented both his ladies and then shyly presented Melissa with a small package tied in silver ribbons. She exclaimed as she opened it to find a small circle brooch of pearls to match the strand she wore around her neck, and kissed him as she thanked him. Aunt

Alice smiled a little thinly until her husband gave her a beautiful fan delicately adorned with chips of emeralds and diamonds, and in perfect amity they went out to the waiting coach.

Melissa was amazed at the number of people who attended the "small" dance; several of the quality had elected to return to town even though the season had not yet begun. She met several other young ladies, and gentlemen who quickly filled her dance card, and as many of Aunt Alice's friends as that lady cared to present, although Melissa found it tiresome to be always introduced as "my sister Anne's daughter; you may not remember her for she was married almost before she came out and she was *so* much older than I!"

Melissa had just joined a group of young people between sets to chat and sip punch when she looked up and saw an elegant gentleman approaching her. She stared, her hand going to her throat, for surely it was the Duke of Colchester! She almost had not recognized him in his evening dress of gray satin, his shapely legs encased in white smallclothes and matching silk stockings, with his shoe buckles tricked out in diamonds. His wig made him look very different, the queue in back concealed in a short black silk bag, but the swarthy face was the same, right down to that devil's grin she remembered so well. She put her punch cup down carefully on a small table near by and tried to disentangle herself from the conversation so she could leave the group, but before she could make good her escape, she heard her uncle's voice saying, "Melissa! May I present a gentleman who begs an introduction? I give you the Duke of Colchester. Tony, my niece, Melissa Ward."

Melissa curtsied and as she rose and gave him her

hand she saw that he was smiling down at her wickedly.

"My pleasure, Miss Ward! But surely we have met before?"

Melissa stared at him uncertainly and withdrew her hand. "I am new arrived in London, sir. I am quite sure we have never met!"

Her eyes dared him to contradict her, but before he could reply, there was a small shriek and Aunt Alice appeared in a whirl of green satin.

"Tony! My dear boy! Where have you been keeping yourself? I would be willing to wager my best brooch that you have been up to no good!"

Tony kissed her hand and said, "Slander, my lady, baseless slander! I have just arrived from Scotland, and it is impossible to be anything *but* good in that location for there is nothing to do there but fish and hunt, and that generally in the rain!" He turned casually to Melissa. "Are you a gambler like your aunt, Miss Ward? She will take *any* wager; perhaps it runs in the family?"

Melissa's eyes flashed as she retorted, "I only bet on sure things, Your Grace! I do not like to lose!"

Aunt Alice broke in again. "La, child, none of us *likes* to! Alas, Tony, my luck has been quite out lately! I have lost at whist times out of number these past weeks. Perhaps I should take up macao!"

Ferdie shuddered and they all laughed, even Aunt Alice who appeared to take the jest in good spirit, so happy as she seemed to see the duke.

When the music began again, Melissa was pleased to see her partner arrive so promptly, but before she could make good her escape the duke insisted on a dance, and then proceeded to mark Lady Throckmorton's card for a waltz, a boulanger, and a set of country dances, until she protested. Melissa left with her escort to the sound of her aunt's tinkling laughter.

"My dear Tony! You will have all the tabbys talking! You are much, much too young for me!"

Melissa could not hear his reply, but her aunt laughed again and playfully tapped his arm with her fan in reproach. Ferdie looked on, seemingly amused by his wife's flirting.

From that moment, the evening was ruined for Melissa. Much as she tried to ignore the duke and appear unconscious, she was constantly aware of him and where he was in the room, and all too soon he came to claim his dance. She was glad she was wearing long kid gloves for she was sure her palms were moist with nervousness. The duke smiled down at her, shamelessly enjoying her confusion.

"How lovely you look this evening, my dear Lissa!" he whispered as he led her onto the floor. "Quite transformed in fact!"

Melissa gave him a scornful glance and refused to answer this compliment. When they met in the set he said, "Of course I suppose I should not compare a highwayman's breeches to debutante white. Tell me, my dear, didn't you feel slightly *outré* there among the innocents, such . . . er . . . such experience as you have had?"

This was so outrageous that Melissa tried to pull away from him, but he held her hand so tightly that she winced.

"Oh, no, my dear, I will have my dance! Remember I gave you fair warning that I intended to win our wager!"

Stung into speech, Melissa gasped, "Do not lose all your money at play, Your Grace! At the end of the year I shall expect a prompt accounting, and you have already lost two months!"

The duke laughed at her. "This promises to be a most interesting season! You are so sure of yourself that you dare to enter my sphere by presenting yourself in town! How brave—and how foolish! I really had grave doubts that I could make you fall in love with me while you were interred at Wardley Hall, but now we are both here . . ."

They were separated by the music again, to Melissa's relief, but when he next took her hand to lead her down the set, he whispered, "I wonder what the Woodsons would say if they knew a common highwayman was gracing their oh so exclusive party?"

For the first time, Melissa smiled. "Surely they would think you were foxed, sir! Who would believe such a Banbury tale? Besides," she added sweetly as the dance ended and she curtsied to him, "I was never a *common* highwayman!"

The duke's eyes sparkled in appreciation as he bowed and led her towards her aunt. She was very conscious of the hard length of him beside her, and his firm hand cupping her elbow. Just as they reached Lady Throckmorton he murmured, "How pleased she seems to see me, don't you agree? I am a great favorite of the lady's and shall definitely encourage the connection. We must meet, oh everywhere, you know!"

On this ominous note he seated her, and after exchanging a few pleasantries with Lady Throckmorton, he bowed and left them. That lady's eyes were dancing as she whispered, "My dear! Your success is assured! Colchester never dances with debutantes, and to single you out thusly sets you above all the other girls! Of course," she added smugly, "it is a compliment to me; he has always admired me! Oh, do look at old Mrs. Greene! What a very odd gown—so English! And why puce?"

Melissa wondered what Aunt Alice would say if she knew the real reason the duke had asked to be presented to her, but she only smiled and nodded. He did not approach her again, but Melissa thought the evening would never end. Happening to glance up once as she was dancing, she caught the duke staring at her, which so confused her that she lost her step. After that she concentrated on the dancing and the conversation of her partners, becoming so vivacious in the process that several men were intrigued with this lovely newcomer. She demurely agreed to receive the morning call of one, and promised to drive in the park with another the following afternoon. At supper, she went down with a group of her new friends, and was pleased to note her seat placed her back to the duke which much increased her enjoyment of the Whitstable oysters and the various other delicacies.

It was very late when Lady Throckmorton declared she had had enough gaiety for one evening and they were able to take their leave. She chatted gaily all the way home for which Melissa was grateful for it allowed her to pursue her own jumbled thoughts. She was abrupt with her maid, dismissing her as soon as she had been undressed. Pacing up and down her room, she pondered the problem. How could she avoid the duke if he were constantly on the scene? She had not bargained for such close contact, and she had been horrified to learn of his close friendship with her aunt and uncle. She had also been unprepared for her response to him, or the fact that his very presence would so disturb her. Tired as

she was, it was a long time before she dropped off to
sleep. She could not banish the memory of a wicked
white grin and a pair of intent dark eyes, and she
still seemed to feel the pressure of his strong hands,
holding hers.

CHAPTER 8

Christmas House Party at Beechwoods

The duke made an appearance at the Throckmortons'
the following morning, but had to be content with
Ferdie's company, for the ladies had gone out. He
enjoyed a glass of excellent Madeira and some aim-
less conversation before he left his compliments and
took himself off to one of his clubs. There was plenty
of time, he thought as he strolled along. He had been
caught unprepared by Melissa's appearance at the
Woodsons' ball, and surprised by his reaction to her.
She had certainly changed! Instead of a dirty urchin
in men's breeches, ('The Young Gentlemen' indeed!),
or the provincial young lady in the tight and faded
habit that he remembered, she had blossomed into a
beauty with her lovely gown and fashionable hairdo;
the equal of any lady of quality. He had not known
she was connected with the Throckmortons and it
put a whole new complexion on things. One did not
play fast and loose with a relative of my Lord

Throckmorton as casually as one did the orphaned daughter of an indigent country gentleman of no title. Perhaps it would be wise to call a halt, but Anthony Northrup had never withdrawn from a wager. Besides, the lady had such sparkling blue eyes, and such a tempting mouth! He was determined to pursue a waiting game and see what fortune was pleased to bestow on him, and put the conquest of Melissa from his mind as he entered Brooks's.

That afternoon, in the perch phaeton of a delighted Mr. Whitney, Melissa smiled and bowed to all her friends, and tried to fend off the more outrageous compliments of her escort. She had chosen to wear a pale green gown and matching pelisse, trimmed in soft gray fur. Her towering hat was adorned with rows of satin ruching and a pair of plumes that swept down one side to frame her face. She knew she looked well; she had taken great pains with her appearance, leading her maid to believe there was a romance in the offing, a fact she did not hesitate to announce belowstairs to an interested audience of servants.

Mr. Whitney was not much older than Melissa and had not conquered a tendency to blush and stammer. This was not due to any diffidence on his part about his station in life; he knew his worth and consequence, and considered himself quite a catch. Why, had not his mama told him so often enough? Melissa was soon heartily bored with him. Such a *boy*, she thought, even as she remembered her aunt's statement that he was worth several thousand a year and would probably outgrow his propensity to corpulence. She was surprised when she found herself thinking that money wasn't everything, after all! Suddenly she stiffened as she saw the Duke of Colchester approaching them on a handsome bay mare, and wished Mr. Whitney were not so quick to check his team at the duke's signal.

He smiled at them both, but Melissa was not deceived. "What a pleasure, Miss Ward; servant, Chauncy!" And then to the startled young man who had more than once been indignant at being ignored by the duke, he added playfully, "I see you have captured the latest Incomparable and managed to persuade her to go for a ride in your carriage too! I am surprised you dared, Miss Ward! I rather thought you would avoid carriage rides for a while!"

Melissa would have spoken, but Mr. Whitney was before her, coloring up and blustering, " 'Pon my word, Your Grace, 'tis perfectly safe! I may not be a member of the Four Horse Club as you are, but I'm a t . . . t . . . tolerable driver! Assure you, Miss Ward, p . . . p . . . perfectly safe with me!"

He seemed so anxious that Melissa might doubt his ability with the ribbons that she gave him a brilliant, reassuring smile.

"I know I am completely safe in your company, sir! To be truthful, I would feel myself in much more danger if the duke were driving me!" This statement was accompanied by another smile, this time aimed directly at the duke, who grinned in appreciation.

"Bravo, Miss Ward, that's won the trick!" he murmured, trying not to laugh as Mr. Whitney hastened to assure Melissa that no one could compare with the finesse and skill of the Duke of Colchester.

"Perhaps you would allow me to demonstrate my expertise some time?" the duke asked her formally, although his dark eyes gleamed with mischief as he bent towards her.

Melissa smoothed her gloves, demurely lowering her lashes. "As to that, m'lord, I must refuse in spite of Mr. Whitney's voucher. I have no desire for it!"

Young Chauncy Whitney began to look bewildered and a little alarmed at the turn of the conversation, for she sounded almost insulting, and he knew the duke to be a warm man, easily offended. He could not help but approve her attitude towards one of London's most notorious rakes, but he was relieved when the duke did not appear to be upset by the put-off, merely saying lightly, "We shall see, shall we not? If you do decide to honor me I can promise you a most interesting and exciting ride!" Melissa blushed angrily as he bowed to them, and tipping his hat, rode away.

Mr. Whitney said knowledgeably, "Must mean his new team. Haven't seen them myself, but understand a bang-up set of sweet goers, and perfectly matched. Trust the duke to have the best!"

Melissa nodded absently, silently congratulating herself on the way she had handled the encounter. That will give him pause, she thought triumphantly, and then catching sight of her escort's doleful expression, realized she should have complimented him on his own team. This omission was speedily rectified and she was treated to a long and boring soliloquy on the merits and bloodlines of the Whitney chestnuts.

December came in with a flurry of snow, and Melissa became accustomed to meetings with the duke. He seemed a constant visitor to the Throckmorton town house, and had the *entrée* to most of the parties she was invited to attend. There was no way she could avoid him! She did not dare tell her aunt of her dislike for his company for she could advance no reasons for it that would bear close scrutiny. Besides, Aunt Alice was in raptures at his attention, although she secretly believed that she was the attraction that kept him in town. What a great thing, she thought in her more noble moments, if she could turn dear Tony's thoughts to her niece! She mentioned it to Ferdie and was surprised to see his frown.

"I cannot like it, my dear," he explained, "I care not for his title or his fortune. I would wish for her a less dissolute, less jaded man! She is so young . . . so innocent. . . ."

His wife interrupted. "Think you so, Ferdie? I would have said she is as shrewd as she can hold together!"

Ferdie sighed. "We are not like to agree on that, my dear, and I must say that I do not think that such a rake as Anthony Northrup would make her happy!"

"Not happy? With the duke? A rake can make a most exciting husband! You do not understand women in the slightest, Ferdie!" Lady Alice tossed her head, looking at him incredulously.

"Alas, I fear you are right, my dear," he said mournfully. "I have yet to understand even one of them . . . you!"

His wife laughed and kissed him lightly, but when he would have tightened his arms around her she whirled away to her desk.

"Now where did I put that list? I know it must be here someplace!" she said, frowning and dropping several bills and invitations to the floor. "Here it is! Now do attend me, Ferdie! Here are the names of the people that I wish to invite to the country."

It was common practice for most of polite society to retire to their estates, or visit friends for the several weeks that comprised the Christmas season, and the Throckmortons were no exception. They generally invited twenty or more companions to help them while away the time. Lady Throckmorton could not abide the boredom and seclusion without some friends to make it more palatable, and a large enough number of them so there was always someone to play cards with, ride with if the weather were pleasant, get up a play or musical entertainment, or just exchange a comfortable coze over the teacups. Lord Throckmorton was agreeable for he knew it made Alice happier, and of course it was a prime object with him to insure her happiness, for if Alice was not happy, no one else was allowed to be either. He was not pleased to see the name of the Duke of Colchester leading all the rest. He knew there was no reason to exclude him if Alice wished for him, but he determined to speak to Melissa about it. He had noticed how stiff and formal she was in Tony's company, almost as if she were afraid of the man, and since Lord Throckmorton was a kind man and genuinely fond of her, he wanted her to feel free to confide in him if she felt she was being pressured in any way.

Melissa had been even more dismayed to see the duke's name as she helped her aunt pen the invitations. Small chance that he would refuse! She had hoped to be relieved of his company during the weeks they would be out of London, and she had been looking forward to being in the country again, seeing Rob and finding out all the news of school and Wardley Hall after all this time. She shrugged philosophically. Since it was not to be after all, she would have to be on her guard. In such a large group of guests she could always be sure of company, and she was pleased to see that Aunt Alice had included several of her particular friends. The list seemed to be divided between the middle-aged and young people in their first season or so. Tony fell between the two stools, and Melissa felt better when she realized that Aunt Alice had probably included him to dance attendance on herself, rather than her niece. She did not give her aunt any credit for possible magnanimous behavior, for she was quite as shrewd as Lady Throckmorton believed.

The journey to Lincoln County took place a week later in crisp, clear weather that easily allowed them to make the fifty miles a day that was considered standard. Melissa rode with her aunt and uncle in the pale blue coach. Most of the servants that would be needed to augment the permanent staff had gone ahead, but m'lord and lady's valet and maid followed in another coach with the trunks and boxes, and they were accompanied also by four outriders who served as guards. No highwayman would dare attack this entourage, Melissa thought, her lips curving in a smile.

Aunt Alice chatted gaily, pleased with her beautiful coach and the magnificent sable cloak that Ferdie had presented to her just before they left town, as an early Christmas gift. He knew she was never so happy as when she was getting out on a new adventure, but he also realized too well that it would not be too many days before the company began to bore her, or the weather depress her, or the quietness of country life bring on her headache spells. He sighed to himself and hoped the guests would amuse her for longer than usual, for he loved his home and was not allowed to spend nearly as much time there as he wished.

Melissa was impressed with Beechwoods, the Throckmorton estate, when they finally drove through a pair of imposing iron gates and up a broad avenue through the home wood. The drive was well-kept and better surfaced than the roads they had been traveling, and when they crossed the last bridge and smartly circled the front, the house itself seemed as large as a castle. Beechwoods was a three-story mansion of gray stone with a wide terrace across the front that faced a sweep of lawn sloping gently to a lake and the woods beyond. There were wings on either side of the main structure that curved outward in a most agreeable manner. The massive front door was thrown open as the coach came to a halt, and bright, welcoming lights streamed towards them as the butler and several footmen came to help them alight. The three of them ate dinner in a dining room that could easily accommodate forty guests, and Melissa was glad that she would have a chance to become familiar with the many enormous rooms and confusing passageways before the rest of the company arrived the following week. She slept soundly in the pretty blue apartment her aunt had chosen for her, glad to be away from the noise and bustle of town, if only for a little while.

Six days later, as she was returning from a ride around the estate with her uncle, she saw the duke's carriage at the front door, and that gentleman just in the act of mounting the shallow steps to the terrace. He turned when he heard their horses and came back down leisurely to greet them. Melissa's heart sank. Her brief respite was over.

The duke was as polished and suave as ever, but she was not deceived, for the devil in his eyes seemed to be saying to her, "Here we are, Lissa . . . together!

The wager is as good as won!" Ferdie shook his hand and asked after the journey.

"Quite comfortable, Ferdie, quite comfortable! I did fear a bit about highwaymen, but we were not stopped. Some of them have grown distressingly bold, you know," he added with a sidelong look at Melissa who stood haughtily next to her uncle, tapping her crop against her shiny black boot.

Before her uncle could reply, she spoke up. "But surely, m'lord, the great Duke of Colchester would never be afraid of a scruffy highwayman! Do you not carry pistols? And employ a guard?"

There was a discreet cough behind her, and she turned to see Minton and Findle, both correctly attired in the duke's livery, waiting for orders. Neither paid her the slightest attention, but she was shocked into silence by their appearance. Surely they recognized her! And even though they were woodenly correct now, what might they say to the other servants? She would have felt a great deal easier if she had known with what an iron hand Colchester ruled his staff. He directed them to unload the trunks and gave some orders to his coachman before he turned back to Melissa and Lord Throckmorton and strolled with them up the steps to the house. The duke smiled kindly at Melissa as he held the door for her, and replying to her last remark said, "As to that, Miss Ward, I have known highwaymen who were not deterred by guards; they are a desperate lot who are not always what they seem. They are, however, notable horsemen—almost as good as you appeared to be, riding up the avenue!"

Uncle Ferdie changed the subject, to Melissa's relief, and she curtsied and excused herself. As she went up the broad stairs to her room, she could feel those bold eyes raking her back, and she kept her head high, glad she had worn the black habit that fitted her so well. She had no intention of succumbing to the duke, but she did not mind in the slightest if he was made aware of what he was missing. She resolved to dress for dinner very carefully, perhaps the new gray gown that was as soft as gossamer, and showed off her shoulders and white neck. . . .

Rob arrived later that day, thrilled to be included in the festivities and somewhat awed to see his sister looking so smart and sophisticated. Melissa rather spoiled the picture by hugging and exclaiming over him under the benevolent smile of the Throckmorton butler, until Rob whispered, "Cut line, Lissa, do! Yes, it is good to see you, but control yourself!" He tugged at his cravat, his color high as Lady Throckmorton swept down the stairs and embraced him. He smiled manfully and thanked her for her kindness in including him while Melissa watched him fondly, thinking how much he had grown and matured since the summer. How handsome he is, she thought, completely unaware of her own beauty and the fact that everyone would know he was her brother with one glance. He was shown to his room, and Melissa did not see him again until dinner time. Aunt Alice had put them together at table, and Melissa was soon catching up on all the news from home. Yes, Aunt Cardell was well, and yes, Lissa's gifts had arrived, and yes, Uncle Ferdie had been as good as his word, and several of the most urgent repairs were already being made.

"Oh, how I envy you, Rob! To have just come from home! I miss Wardley so much!"

Rob looked around the magnificent dining hall, the brilliant company so richly dressed, the candlelight glowing on the array of crystal and plate and hothouse flowers, and the liveried footmen behind every chair. "Miss Wardley Hall?" he asked incredulously. "When you can be *here*? You're all about in your head, Lissa!"

She had to laugh at what she knew was a typical sentiment from her worldly brother, and the duke who happened to glance down the long table in their direction thought he had never seen such a handsome young pair or ever seen Melissa looking quite so beautiful as she did this evening. It caused him a small pang to realize that he had never been able to bring a smile of delight and such a loving expression to her face, and that when she was forced to converse with him, her features grew still and wary and distrustful. On his left, Lady Throckmorton asked him if he thought the weather would hold for a proposed riding expedition the following morning, and he reluctantly turned his thoughts from the elusive Miss Ward.

When the gentlemen rejoined the ladies, he knew a bit more about Melissa's young brother. The boy had tried hard to be unobtrusive and retiring, but under the duke's skillful questioning and the token glass of port his uncle had poured him, he became quite communicative. Tony thought him a silly young cub who was bound to fall into several scrapes before he reached maturity; he detected the nature of a true gamester as well, and decided that the odds were high that Master Rob would follow the same road as his father before him, but that was not Anthony Northrup's concern, thank heavens!

As he entered the drawing room, he saw Melissa had surrounded herself with Mary Wilcox and her bosom-bow Miss Clark, and that the three of them soon attracted all the younger gentlemen like magnets. From his seat amongst the dowagers the duke watched Melissa flirting lightly. Lord Marshall languidly challenged him to a game of billiards, and several of the guests decided to watch the match. The duke caught Melissa's relieved eyes as he left the room, and he smiled in amusement. Did she really think he would attempt to make love to her in a crowded drawing room, under so many aristocratic noses? He dispatched Lord Marshall quickly, and accepted Ferdie's challenge. When the tea tray appeared in the drawing room, and the gentlemen again rejoined the ladies, Tony went to the sofa where Lady Throckmorton was sitting and made himself agreeable, ignoring Melissa completely. Somehow that infuriated her, and she was in a distinctly bad mood when she took up her bedroom candle with the other ladies and prepared to retire. The duke caught her eye and winked at her, and she turned hastily and climbed the stairs.

The weather held the next morning; indeed it was unseasonably warm for late December, and most of the house party were gathered on the terrace waiting for the grooms to bring the horses from the stables. Melissa was wearing her black habit and a new riding hat, daringly severe for a miss in her first season but most becoming with its scarf of white chiffon. She had bent her head over a wayward button on her tight glove and was not aware of the duke until he stepped up beside her and took her hand.

"Allow me, Miss Ward," he said calmly, and proceeded to button her black glove for her. "Why is it that you ladies have so many of these infernal little things? It must take you an age to remove the long kid gloves you wear to a ball!" Melissa shivered at his touch, and saw a muscle twitch by the corner of his mouth in amusement as he felt her reaction to his nearness.

She forced herself to stand completely still until he had finished. "I thank you, Your Grace," she said steadily enough. "I am sure you also have found buttons troublesome on many occasions!" She blushed scarlet as he put back his head and laughed out loud, and prayed that none of the other guests had heard her *faux pas*. Why, oh why, did she always say the wrong things?

The duke bent towards her and whispered, "But if they annoy me, m'dear, I merely ignore them!" His bold eyes raked her figure, one black eyebrow quirked. Melissa suddenly felt that he could see right through the black habit, and was reliving the memory of her helpless and bound in his coach, or locked in his room at the Running Fox. She backed away from him, inadvertently raising her whip, now as white as she had been red a moment before. Tony bowed.

"Relax, my dear Lissa! There are at least fifteen people joining us on this ride, and if you do not let your superior horsemanship carry you away, you can remain safely in the group. And that is a shame! Captain notwithstanding, my bay could give you a race! Do you care for *another* wager, Miss Ward?"

Melissa looked around to make sure that no one was in earshot, and then she said in a small voice, "Sir, shall we disregard that silly wager? I should be glad to release you from it if you will only agree."

The duke folded his arms, his eyes narrowing slightly. "Are you afraid of losing, Miss Ward? No, I do not wish to be 'released' from the wager, for, you see, I quite look forward to the winning of it. Each time I see you I am more determined on a successful conclusion!"

Melissa frowned at him. "But I have no intention of allowing you to win it, Your Grace, no intention at all! I merely suggested it to spare you disappointment!" She raised her head as Tony laughed again, and moved away from him as Findle brought him his horse and gave her a knowing glance. She hurried to Mary's side until Captain was fetched and tried hard to discourage Mary's whispered questions about the duke and their conversation. Her friend seemed to think her fortunate to have captured Colchester's interest, and Melissa shuddered. "Interest" was not the word she would have chosen to describe his attention!

All morning long she rode gently with her aunt and some of the older gentlemen, laughingly refusing Rob's challenge to a race across one of the brown winter fields. Chauncy Whitney stayed doggedly by her side, a perfect watchdog she realized, as she caught the duke's amused eyes. If only he did not remind her so much of a fat sheepdog, jealously guarding a lamb! When she dismounted for luncheon she had the happy thought that almost half the year was over, and felt immeasurably better. Surely she could outwit the duke for the remaining months of the wager, even if it meant encouraging Mr. Whitney to hang on her sleeve, or constantly surrounding herself with the other young ladies and their beaux. And there were the elderly gentlemen too, who had shown such a kind interest in her and whose stories tended to be extremely lengthy . . . yes, all in all she was sure she could outwit the duke, and she went up to change with a much brighter outlook towards the future.

That afternoon, Aunt Alice summoned her to her boudoir where she was resting before the evening's activities. Lady Throckmorton was not pleased with her niece. Not only had she seen Melissa ignoring Mr. Whitney to converse with the Earl of Somerset who must be all of sixty-five and a grandfather many times over, she had also observed her in the little *tête-à-tête* with the Duke of Colchester. He should have been admiring *her* soft rose habit, trimmed with ermine, and making *her* outrageous compliments in his soft, lazy drawl, his dark eyes sparkling with innuendo. Instead she had been forced to converse with General Adams, quite her most elderly flirt. Her mouth turned down in a pout. It was too bad! After all she had done for Robert's daughter! She tartly reminded her niece that the house party was a marvelous opportunity to ensure that some gentleman fixed his interest on her. When they returned to London, she added spitefully, Melissa would find that she was considered nothing out of the common way compared to some of the reigning beauties. Melissa bent her head and let the storm of petulance wash over her. She had no intention of allowing Mr. Whitney to propose, for she knew very well that that was what her aunt was alluding to. If he did, he would get a kindly but firm refusal. She was confused, for surely he was the answer to all Wardley's problems, but somehow she could not make herself consider him. There must be someone else, she thought wildly, whom I would not dislike so much and whom I could learn to tolerate. She put any thought of love firmly from her mind; that was too much to ask, but a lifetime of Mr. Whitney's earnest, boring conversation and air of self-importance, to say nothing of his waddling walk and fat face, was a sacrifice too great to be considered. Why, oh why, did she keep seeing the duke's firm, sensuous mouth and crisp, black hair in her mind's eye? And why did she imagine she could still feel the pressure of his strong fingers on her wrist when he had buttoned her glove? And wonder of wonders, why had she smoothed the glove so carefully as she removed it, and even held it to her cheek for a moment? She took a deep breath and realized her aunt had stopped speaking and was looking at her angrily.

"Indeed, Aunt Alice," she said hastily, "I know you are right, and I will try to follow your advice, but to be truthful, I have no feelings of affection for Mr. Whitney, nor would I if he had twice as much wealth. He is fat and boring and conceited to boot!"

Her aunt stared at her in amazement. "What does that matter? Marriage with a Whitney would insure your comfort and the restoration of Wardley! That is what you want, is it not, miss? I do hope you are not thinking that you must be in love as well!" She laughed scornfully, and Melissa blushed.

"Indeed no, Aunt, but I must have some feeling of affection. . . . I mean, I cannot marry for the money alone. How vastly unfair to Mr. Whitney! I am sure you did not marry Uncle Ferdie just for his money!" she replied hotly, and then realized that she had gone too far. She stole a worried glance at her aunt and was surprised to see her blushing as she turned the rings on her fingers absently. Lady Throckmorton was remembering how and why she had chosen Ferdie from among her many suitors, and had the grace to be a little embarrassed. Since her own sister had stolen Robert Ward, yes, stolen him away when she *knew* how Alice felt about him, she was determined to best her by marrying the wealthiest husband she could find. If she could not have her beloved Robert, what did it matter whom she wed? Of course, she reassured herself hastily, it had all worked out for the best in the end, and she had grown quite fond of dear Ferdie over the years. And if her heart had never beat as fast for him as it had for Robert, at least now she was not an impoverished widow, forced to live in a ruined country manor, and saddled with three children to boot! Recalling Melissa suddenly, she dismissed her with only a brief word of warning to watch what she was about, for there were too few young men wealthy enough not to care about marrying a penniless girl.

Melissa went slowly back to her room, deep in thought. She was quiet all through dinner, and would have been amazed to know that her most ardent suitor was silently applauding her modesty and demeanor. Surely his mama would be pleased with Miss Ward even though she had reminded him countless times how difficult it would be to find someone worthy enough to suit them both! He wished she were here so she could see for herself what a paragon he had chosen! He smiled at Melissa as he sat across from her at table, and was unaware that she was looking right through him.

In the drawing room, Lord Marshall asked the Throckmortons if they would have any objections to the guests performing a short play he had brought with him. Aunt Alice smiled at him approvingly, and assured him it would be prodigious amusing, already planning to play the major role. She agreed to see to the costumes, flattered by Lord Marshall's statement that only her exquisite taste would suffice. Sure that he had spiked the lady's theatrical ambitions, and unaware that Lady Throckmorton planned to delegate all the work to the already overburdened servants, subject to her approval of course, Lord Marshall himself offered to direct the play and be in charge of such props as were necessary. The other guests began to discuss the play and there was so much interest in this new amusement that Lord Marshall called for a reading first thing in the morning, insisting everyone must try for a part. Melissa was wondering how to avoid participating, for she had never acted in her life, when Mr. Whitney said in a pompous aside, "I am sure *you* have no desire for it, Miss Ward. You are much too modest, too retiring, to put yourself forward in such an unladylike way. . . ." He beamed at her possessively and with such a calm air of knowing what was best for her, that Melissa was angered.

"But you are wrong, Mr. Whitney!" she retorted. "I should enjoy it of all things, and since my aunt and uncle endorse the proposal, I hardly think that I will be overstepping any of society's rules of behavior!"

"Bravo!" the duke applauded, as Mr. Whitney stared at her in dismay. "I am sure you would make a perfect heroine, or perhaps if Percy should find himself short of qualified actors, you might try for a male role? Somehow I can see you carrying even that off with aplomb!"

Melissa refused to be drawn into answering this sally, and turned abruptly to ask Lord Marshall the plot of the play.

Mr. Whitney scowled at the duke over his teacup and decided it was just as well that his mama had been forced to go to Aunt Agatha's for Christmas, due to that lady's failing health, for he firmly intended to join the theatrical party too if Miss Ward was to be among their numbers. He was horrified at his daring for he knew his mama's nice notions of gentility, and he could imagine all too well her reaction to the news that her beloved Chauncy was about to become a common player! He wiped his brow and was glad some three hundred miles separated the lady from Beechwoods!

CHAPTER 9

Amateur Theatricals

Percy Marshall had all the appearance of a fop, concerned only with the intricate folds of his cravats, his numerous canes and snuff boxes, and the excellent fit of his coats. He was taller than average, and thin, but this and his high complexion and wavy brown hair were quite unremarkable when compared with his really magnificent beak of a nose. He appeared languid in conversation and careless in demeanor, but in reality he had a sharp mind and a quick turn of phrase. A close friend of the Duke of Colchester, he had known my Lord and Lady Throckmorton forever, and sincerely hoped that by appointing the lady costume designer, he might keep her from aspiring to the major role. It would be ludicrous for a woman her age, he thought cynically, no matter how carefully preserved, to attempt a girl of eighteen, but he would not have bet a ha'penny that that wasn't what she fully expected to do. She seemed to feel she was forever frozen at that age, and although her years were obvious to the polite world, she refused to acknowledge them. He had already decided her beautiful niece was perfect for the part if she had any acting ability at all, and when Lady Throckmorton joined him early in the morning room, he sighed gently, well aware of stormy weather ahead. She rarely made an appearance this early; it could only be because of the readings, but he allowed none of his chagrin to show on his face as he rose and made her an elegant leg.

"My dear Percy, you see me in attendance as you requested! Am I the first?" she asked gaily, favoring him with a bright smile.

Lord Marshall returned the smile gamely. "Lady Throckmorton, lovely as usual! You show all our younger ladies such a marvelous example, for that cherry silk becomes you mightily! I am sure they must be discouraged when they compare their toilettes to yours; but then they do not realize how many years are required before such perfection can be acquired!"

He led her to a seat, ignoring her pout and sudden frown. "Besides," he added, "there was no need for you to put yourself to the trouble, for I doubt very much that we will get to a discussion of costumes today!"

Lady Throckmorton drew a deep breath and would have spoken, but Mary Wilcox entered just then, followed closely by Agnes Clark and Melissa. The girls were laughing together and greeted Lord Marshall and Lady Throckmorton cheerfully. Melissa sensed that all was not well; she had seen that pinched look on her aunt's face before, and as well as Uncle Ferdie, knew it boded no good. She was relieved when Mary went to compliment her aunt on her dress, although she wondered why the lady did not look more pleased, or why her manner was so aloof as she greeted the other guests when they appeared.

Not everyone was interested in performing. Uncle Ferdie had declared he would only attempt to play first audience, but he promised to applaud loudly, and some of the other older ladies and gentlemen had long since given up any pretensions to acting, even at a house party among friends. Melissa hoped the duke would also disdain the venture, and her heart sank as she saw him enter the room and exchange a few words with Lord Marshall. Mr. Whitney bustled in behind him and hurried to take a seat near Melissa. He mopped his brow nervously as he confessed he had never taken part in such a thing; he wondered still if it were quite the thing and what his mama would say if she knew about it, and then he hoped he would not have many lines to learn, until Melissa grew wearied with him and turned away to send a welcoming smile to her brother, standing diffidently near the door. Lord Marshall called the company to order and proceeded to outline the play. It was a slight vehicle at best, but it had the advantage of a number of characters, only three of them with many lines to learn. The heroine was a young girl, torn between two suitors, a London beau and her childhood sweetheart from the country. The beau would captivate her before she realized his nefarious intentions, which did not include marriage, of course. Before the final curtain she would realize her mistake and be rescued by her gallant rural swain. Lord Marshall asked the young ladies to read first, and as he had expected, Melissa was by far the best. Although she tried to read indifferently, there was really no choice, for Mary Wilcox could not control her giggle, and Miss Clark declared in her somewhat piercing nasal voice that she could never remember lines—it was quite out of the question! Studiously ignoring Lady Throckmorton's angry eyes and tapping foot, Lord Marshall gave the lead to Melissa and assigned the others to play her friends and guests at a ball that figured in the second act. He did not ask Lady Throckmorton to play a secondary role, for he knew full well that she had to be the star or nothing! Alan Cranston was chosen to play the country lover. He had an open, easy manner and he spoke his lines firmly and well, admitting to the applause that he had "had a go" at acting when he was up at Cambridge. Melissa looked around the room. The villain still had to be chosen, and somehow she did not think Lord Marshall would choose her brother to play a hardened rake, and certainly Mr. Whitney was out of the question! That left Mr. Wellbank who stuttered, and Lord Evans who at fifty and with a game leg hardly filled the part of a dashing Corinthian. And of course the Duke of Colchester. Her heart sank as she saw Lord Marshall hand him a script which he tried to refuse. "Oh, surely, Percy, this is too much!"

Lord Marshall was relentless. "You will be perfect for the part, Tony. Why, you only have to play yourself, after all!"

"Thank you so much, my dear," the duke said dryly, turning over the pages, one black eyebrow raised. "I will not have a shred of reputation left if any of my set hear about this . . . especially if I have to utter such a line as this!—

Now my fair beauty, resign yourself to your

fate, for you will be mine before the cock crow
again!

Good heavens, is this a comedy then?"

The guests laughed at his expression of supercilious
hauteur, and begged him to take the part. With a sidelong glance at Melissa's horrified face he allowed
himself to be persuaded, and the rest of the roles
were quickly assigned. Mr. Whitney found himself
the butler, much to his disgust, and was only molli-
fied when Lord Marshall pointed out that he would
be on stage most of the time, but would only have a
few lines to learn. The first rehearsal was set for
that afternoon, Lord Marshall ordering it for "principals only, this time, company!" which sounded so
professional that the duke asked him if sometime in
his past he had not trod the boards himself, at
Haymarket or Drury Lane? The guests went into
luncheon laughing and discussing the play, and if
Chauncy Whitney was red in the face and seemed to
frown a great deal, and if Lady Throckmorton was
unusually silent and distant, no one seemed to notice.

Melissa fled to her room after the meal, as much to
avoid Mr. Whitney as the duke, who to his credit
showed no desire to seek her out or bother her with
excessive attentions. He seemed to be deriving a
great deal of amusement from her rotund suitor
however, as Melissa found out when she went
reluctantly to the library that afternoon for the first
rehearsal. Mr. Whitney was not only present, he was
determined to remain, even though Lord Marshall
assured him there was no need for his attendance.
The duke's eyes gleamed with suppressed laughter,
and young Alan Cranston looked bewildered until
he saw the proprietary way Mr. Whitney led Melissa

to a seat next to him at the big oak library table where the others were waiting. Melissa thanked him distantly as Lord Marshall suggested they read the play through together to get a feel for it, and soon forgot her annoyance at Mr. Whitney's possessive air as the story unfolded. The first scene was with Mr. Cranston at her country home, and the two of them read the lines easily, Mr. Cranston stumbling only a little at the histrionics when he begged the fair Rosamunde to forego her trip to London and promise to marry him instead. Lord Marshall took all the other parts; a maid, Rosamunde's doughty grandmother and a lady caller, and his change of voice for each character soon had them all laughing in earnest. He smiled sweetly at them, and said he did not mind them being amused; he took it as a compliment to his expertise. Mr. Whitney read his lines loudly, but unfortunately seemed to feel a lower-class accent was necessary. "Ass!" muttered Lord Marshall to the duke. "I only chose him since his natural pomposity is perfect for the part of an upper-class butler! Starched-up, stupid and superior!" Aloud, he commended Mr. Whitney to closely observe the Throckmorton butler as an excellent guide to his performance.

The second act was the ballroom scene where the lady meets the rake, and the duke threw himself into the part nobly, inspired no doubt by Percy Marshall's performance. Melissa blushed at some of her lines, and at a particularly provocative statement, she happened to glance up at the duke and found him smiling at her, obviously enjoying himself immensely. She stopped in mid-sentence. When everyone looked at her inquiringly, she stammered, "What a horrible flirt your fair Rosamunde is, Lord

Marshall! Is it really necessary to simper and be so coy? And tapping him with my fan! I would never behave so under any circumstances!" Lord Marshall assured her she would soon become accustomed, and the reading continued. In the third act, when all was going at a great pace, Melissa missed her cue again. The country beau had now appeared in town to try and win her hand again, and during his long impassioned plea, she had peeked ahead to the next scene. It took place in a hunting box to which the rake had taken her by force, despairing of winning her any other way. The color drained from her face as she read some of the lines, and it was not until she realized that all the men were staring at her again that she turned back hastily and tried to recover her composure.

" 'Alas, Roger,' " she read tonelessly, " 'I fear your impetuosity does you no good. Please to rise, you are distressing me.' "

Lord Marshall broke in. "A little more feeling, I think, Miss Ward, and perhaps you might weep a little in girlish confusion as you deny him? With a large handkerchief much in evidence, that should do it! You do not want to hurt the poor boy's feelings after all!"

The actors continued through the kidnapping scene, Melissa's color fading, and her voice getting fainter and fainter. Lord Marshall's expressive eyebrows rose, and he looked wildly at the duke who winked at him. Mr. Cranston continued his part with a long speech about rescuing the lady from her vile abductor. "I say!" he exclaimed, tossing down his script, "I agree with Miss Ward, this is a lot of silliness! I cannot imagine any *real* person speaking some of these lines!"

The others laughed, the tension broken, although Mr. Whitney still looked very stern and disapproving. "Well, my dear," Lord Marshall drawled, "we may play it for a comedy if you like. I did not feel we were up to Shakespeare, and this playlet has the edifying lesson of virtue triumphant at the end; such a nice touch in these dissolute times, don't you agree?"

"And so seldom found in real life," the duke agreed, turning the pages. "I see I am to be thoroughly dispatched, in fact killed by your superior sword-play, Alan! I shall try to lie very still so as not to interrupt your final touching scene with the lady, although in real life I am sure I could write quite a different ending!"

Mr. Cranston agreed with him. "Oh, aye, Your Grace, no question about that! But then, I would not be so foolhardy as to challenge you to a duel!" He bowed hastily to Melissa, as if he felt she might be offended by such heartfelt sentiments. He knew the duke's skill!

It was late afternoon when the reading ended. Melissa lost no time in retiring, with Mr. Whitney in close attendance, and Mr. Cranston also wandered away in search of other amusements. Lord Marshall and the duke stayed by the fire, talking desultorily of this and that, until Lord Marshall recalled Melissa's behavior, and questioned his friend.

"Whatever is the matter with the beauteous Miss Ward?" he asked lazily. "I thought she was about to faint towards the end! You haven't been frightening her, have you, Tony? Lord, 'twould be like shooting ducks in a basket if *you* were after her!"

Tony stretched his long legs to the fire and inspected the tassel on his boot before he replied carelessly, "I do not think the lady cares for me, Percy, and the thought of the stolen kiss she will be required to deny me is probably preying on her mind!"

"That must make a nice change for you, my dear!" Lord Marshall replied. "Quite a set-down, in fact!"

Tony grinned at him, not at all discomforted by the sarcasm. "Perhaps by the time of the performance I shall have . . . hmm . . . induced her to change her mind! I don't feel I have any *serious* competition from the pompous Mr. Whitney, after all!"

Lord Marshall straightened the pages of the script and frowned a little. "Take care what you are about, dear boy! There are harder ways to find yourself in parson's mousetrap! She is, after all, Lord Throckmorton's niece, and I do not think he would care for any of your hubble-bubble tricks with one of his relatives!"

"Yes, that is bothersome, but I can assure you, my dear Percy," his friend said slowly, "that marriage is not at all on my mind, and I have no intention of being trapped in it. Lord, you know me better than that!"

He seemed unusually vehement, and Lord Marshall hastened to return a light answer. He continued with a tart appraisal of Chauncy Whitney's acting abilities, and the two were soon strolling out arm in arm in laughing accord in response to the first dressing bell.

Between the play rehearsals, the chores Aunt Alice gave her to do, and trying to keep both Mr. Whitney and the duke at arm's length, Melissa found the days speeding by. She had less time to spend with her brother than she would have liked, and worried a little when she saw how taken he was with some of the younger gamesters. He was always ready to play at cards, and she knew very well that some of the stakes were high, but when she tried to remonstrate with him, he became angry and told her in no uncertain terms that he could manage his own life, thank you very much, and was not quite such a lamb for the fleecing as she seemed to think! In fact, if she must know, he was well ahead of the game!

The weather turned much colder, and one morning the guests awoke to a snow-filled world, the wind blowing strongly, and thick, white flakes falling steadily and blotting out the landscape. Now the play became even more important, for no one could go for rides, or walks in the gardens and grounds. Melissa was often in the ballroom where a small stage had been hastily erected, helping her aunt's dresser with costume alterations, or asking the footmen to bring such items of furniture as Lord Marshall demanded for his sets. Aunt Alice had washed her hands of the whole performance since she was not to have the lead, and was pettish with Ferdie. He feared that she would want to be off to London the moment she could manage to sweep the last guest from the house, and his heart sank. One evening, he begged her to sing for their guests, and there was so much applause, and so many fulsome compliments that she was appeased, especially when one of the younger and more impressionable guests wrote a poem dedicated to a golden-haired nightengale. Since he neglected to sign it, she was intrigued by the mystery, and spent a lot of time trying to decide who it might be. Ferdie had no objections and rather hoped the poet would write another to her big blue eyes, if it would only keep Alice amused!

The duke kept his distance from Melissa, except on the stage of course, and treated her with such a

teasing lightness that she began to feel much more
at ease in his presence. She began to hope that
whatever tactics he planned to try and make her fall
in love with him and thus win their wager, he would
not attempt them as a guest in her uncle's home for
he seemed to have some of the attributes of a gentleman!

One evening Aunt Alice had planned an especially festive dinner to be followed by a small dance
to which she invited all the notables in the immediate neighborhood. She herself could not stand the
vicar and his wife, or the local squires and their
dowdy consorts, but it seemed to please Ferdie, and
outside the big harvest festival for the tenant farmers
that was held on the grounds in late September, she
did not have to see any of the locals from one year to
the next. She made a special point to dress in her
finest, to give the provincials a treat as she put it.
Melissa thought she looked overdressed and over-
jeweled, but Ferdie was proud of her and beamed as
he stood beside her to greet the guests, whispering
the names that she had never bothered to remember.

The ballroom had been decorated in greens and
holly, and bright red velvet ribbons, and all the
chandeliers sparkled with red candles in honor of
the season. Aunt Alice had insisted that Melissa
wear a new gown of red velvet to carry out the decor.
It was cut even lower than her other gowns and she
was distinctly uncomfortable in it, especially when
she saw the duke raise his quizzing glass in her
direction, and then one mobile black eyebrow.

When the musicians began, she found him before
her, bowing and asking for the first dance. She had
hoped he would feel he had to ask Aunt Alice, but
Ferdie was leading his wife out, and Mr. Whitney

was glaring at the duke, so she had no choice but to assent as graciously as she could, and give him her hand. Aunt Alice had bid the musicians strike up a waltz, a daring move in the country, and one that quite scandalized all the local ladies, which of course was just what she had in mind. Melissa felt the duke's strong arm around her waist, holding her closer than necessary, as his other hand clasped hers warmly and he smiled down at her. She felt breathless with his nearness, but she was determined he should know nothing about it.

"May I tell you how very lovely you look this evening, my dear Lissa?" he murmured in her ear. "Red velvet and black hair compliment each other so well, to say nothing of the generous expanse of cream! I see Mr. Whitney is frowning at us! Can it be that he disapproves of me? Or your neckline? Or the both together in such close proximity?" She glanced over the duke's arm as he whirled her to the music, and saw Mr. Whitney leaning against the wall, glowering and sulking and almost laughed out loud. Her amusement was short-lived, however, as the duke continued, "I do *so* hope you will not feel you have to solve your problems by marrying the young idiot! You did say you would do *anything* to save Wardley Hall, did you not? But surely such a noble sacrifice would be too much!"

She looked up at him startled, and was surprised to see an intent look in those dark eyes that belied his light, teasing tones. She was about to reply when he continued, "Of course, Chauncy is worth several thousand a year; as rich as Golden Ball in fact, and that must be a prime consideration with you, I am sure!"

Melissa stiffened. How dare he insult her by imag-

ining she would do such a thing? The duke continued dancing excellently and she had to admit to
herself that marriage to Mr. Whitney would solve
all her problems, if only she had the heart for it.
When the dance ended, she still had not spoken a
word, but swept him a deep curtsey and imperiously
extended her hand. His eyes sparkled as he bowed
over it. "What a shame if you do decide to have him!
All that regality wasted on a mere mister!" He put
her hand on his arm and led her from the floor, and
then he added, "One more thought before you decide,
my dear. Do consider the children! One could not
hope that they would all resemble their mother, and
although I have observed that mothers are especially partial to their offspring for reasons that escape the rest of us mere mortals, I find it hard to
imagine you coddling and beaming over a miniature
Chauncy!"

Melissa longed to slap him as he squeezed her
hand and laughed as he released it and turned her
over to the gentleman he had just been victimizing.
Mr. Whitney was not happy as he led Melissa into
the set just forming. Although he himself was no
dancer, and considered the waltz immoral, it had not
pleased him at all to see her held so closely by the
Duke of Colchester, and being expertly swirled around
the floor. Besides, although he was much struck
with her gown, he could not feel it would meet his
mama's approval. He had not thought Miss Ward
capable of such immodesty, and had a sudden qualm
that perhaps he had been wrong in his assessment of
her maidenly qualities. But when they met in the
dance, and went down the row together, she smiled
at him so sweetly he soon put such ignoble thoughts
from his mind. Of course she had to be gracious to

her aunt's guests, that was all. And she was so beautiful! If he had known the brilliant smile was for the duke's benefit, standing with the Throckmortons and watching her dancing, he would have been aghast. He decided that Miss Ward would soon settle down after marriage, and become as proper and staid as he was himself. He was sure his mama would be delighted to help her!

The duke asked Melissa to dance again, but made no more mention of Mr. Whitney, to her relief. She danced as well with Percy Marshall and Alan Cranston who admitted ruefully that he hoped he was a better actor than a dancer and said he would try very hard not to step on her, but he made no promises. Rob even asked his sister for a dance, and she was delighted. Aunt Alice sighed and smiled as she saw them laughing together, and the duke, who was dancing with her, asked for an explanation.

"So much like their dear father, the Wards! I am overcome each time I see them together! He was the handsomest man, and Rob is the image of him! Oh, I am so glad Ferdie insisted—I mean agreed that I should sponsor them!" The duke smiled and said nothing but his eyes followed the vision in red all evening.

The guests awoke the next morning to light snow. The play was soon to be performed, and Lord Marshall called for many more rehearsals to be sure everyone knew their part. That morning, the actors assembled early in the ballroom where last night they had danced. The servants had removed all traces of the festivities, and the stage, which only last night had held the musicians, was once again ready for the players. Melissa was letter-perfect in her part, and seldom had to be cued, unless Tony insisted on inserting a few lines of his own devising which he did on occasion. Lord Marshall quickly restored him to order.

After a final dress rehearsal two days later, he pronounced them to be as ready as they ever would be, and that evening at dinner invited all the other guests to the performance to be held the following night.

Ferdie insisted on inviting some of the local neighbors who had attended the dance, and allowed the servants to look on from the rear of the ballroom, so it was a good-sized crowd that assembled to see the amateur theatricals. Melissa was surprised that she was not in the least nervous, although Miss Clark had palpitations, and Mr. Whitney looked worried as he mumbled his few lines over and over. When everyone was seated in the darkened ballroom, two footmen slowly drew the makeshift curtains apart. It went very well. There was applause and laughter at the right moments, the duke was suitably sinister, Melissa girlishly appealing, and Mr. Cranston nobly determined. The curtain closed on the first act to bravos and applause, and the actors settled down to have as good a time as their audience. During the third act when the duke held Rosamunde captive, he slipped in an allusion to highwaymen, and a line about hopeless wagers. Melissa was fully prepared for a sudden change of lines, or an outrageous statement, so she answered him easily, although her eyes gleamed angrily.

At last the time came for him to seize her in his arms and attempt to kiss her. During rehearsals, she had been allowed to repulse him, but now he ignored the script, and bending his head, kissed her very slowly and thoroughly. She could not help but remember the last time as she felt his lips on hers, warm and thrilling, and the helplessly lovely feeling of being imprisoned in his strong arms. She was unaware of the murmurs from the audience, or a startled exclamation from offstage. Alan Cranston bounded forward, propelled by Mr. Whitney, and although he was startled, manfully gave his first line as he pulled Melissa away from the duke. She put both hands up to her face horrified, which Lord Marshall thought was much the best performance she had given all evening!

Before long, the two men were engaged in their mock duel, with Melissa wishing spitefully that Mr. Cranston really would run the villain through, instead of just pretending to! After the duke was thoroughly vanquished, the lovers reunited, and the curtain pulled together, the applause was loud and long. The duke rose to his feet, ignoring Melissa's angry face as he dusted himself off casually, and then the three principals went before the curtain, Melissa between the two men, to bow to the audience.

Everyone agreed they had done a superlative job, and Lord Throckmorton called for champagne to celebrate. Soon even Aunt Alice was smiling and accepting compliments on her niece, the costumes, and her liberality in allowing the play to be performed. Melissa stayed close to her uncle, and was so quiet and subdued that not even Chauncy Whitney could fault her. He kept well away from her, however, wishing he could call the duke out one moment, and the next declaring himself well out of it, for such immodest behavior indicated an unsteady temperament. She must have encouraged the duke for him to take such a liberty! He could imagine his mama's reaction if she could have seen his soon-to-be betrothed being publicly and passionately kissed on a stage before an audience!

Melissa thought the evening would never end, and hastily made her excuses as soon as the invited guests left the house. She said she was tired after all the excitement, and Uncle Ferdie hugged her and told her to sleep late in the morning.

Instead of going to bed, however, Melissa paced up and down her room before the dying fire, reliving the moment on stage, and wondering what on earth she was to do now? It had all brought back the first kiss so vividly, and she had sensed under the provocative teasing that made the duke actually embrace her, a kind of stern determination on his part. He had not given up the wager! Oh, no, his mouth seemed to say as it closed over hers, you will love me at last! She shivered a little, still feeling his strong arms and fast-beating heart so close to hers. For one crazy moment she had wanted him to sweep her up and carry her away—from the play, from her aunt and uncle—from all the other guests. What on earth was the matter with her? He did not mean to marry her she knew, and it was not love he felt for her. After he won the wager, he would walk away without a backward glance. She stood up straighter and clenched her fists. She did not love him, she told herself fiercely! He was so careless, so scornful of the feelings of others, such a *rake!* Why, she pitied his wife, whoever she might someday be! He would leave her with a parcel of children while he amused himself just as he always had, making other young girls fall in love with him whenever he fancied them. But not Melissa Ward, Your

Grace, she said to herself. Oh, no, I will never give in, never!

She summoned her maid and was soon in bed, determined to forget him, but it was a long time before she was able to sleep.

CHAPTER 10

Enter Lord Warner;
Rob's Confession

The performance of the play seemed to signal the end of the house party, and it was not many more days before the guests began taking their leave. The duke was one of the first to go, with his friend Lord Marshall. He had made no further moves towards Melissa who avoided him whenever possible, although one evening she looked up to see him contemplating her across the drawing room with an intent, speculative stare. She looked away hastily, wondering if he was regretting that impetuous stage kiss, or feeling a little guilty about his behavior. He was formally correct when he bid her and the Throckmortons good-bye, and drove away down the snowy drive.

Melissa found herself missing the play rehearsals; a game of cards, an afternoon spent with her aunt and the other ladies working on needlepoint, or walks with her friends on the garden paths seemed suddenly flat and boring. Aunt Alice was impatient to be back in town, and made no secret of it. Even the most thick-skinned of her guests were soon making plans for departure. Rob went back to school, and Melissa felt sad when she saw him ride away. He had been so subdued, so quiet towards the end of his stay that if she had not had the duke so much on her mind, she would have been alarmed. To Rob's relief, she did not question him, just hugged him hard, with tears in her eyes. When would she see him again? Not for many months at best, although she promised to be back at Wardley when he came home for the summer holidays.

Chauncy Whitney had been solemn and reserved since the play, and Melissa could only be glad that one good thing had come of her debut as an actress; her unwanted but persistent suitor had withdrawn. He made no secret of the fact that he was displeased with her behavior. Even Aunt Alice was amused. "Who would have thought that he would take it that way?" she asked Ferdie and Melissa at the dinner table the evening before their own departure for town. "I was sure he was about to ask for your hand, Melissa! How starched-up and silly! 'Twas only a play after all!"

Ferdie frowned as he caught sight of Melissa's strained, white face. "You should rather be angry at Tony, my dear! Alan Cranston let slip that that fatal kiss was not in the script. Whatever was Tony thinking of?"

Aunt Alice laughed. "How could he resist the opportunity, and when did he ever not take every advantage if he could? Should we insist he marry Melissa to save her good name?"

She gurgled with laughter at the thought, and

Melissa dropped her soup spoon with a clatter. "Please do not, Uncle!" she implored him. "I would never marry such a man, never!"

Uncle Ferdie patted her hand. "Do not worry, my dear, your aunt is only funning. There can be no question of your marrying anyone that you do not wish to, especially the Duke of Colchester!" Uncle Ferdie looked almost fierce, and Melissa was relieved.

When the Throckmortons arrived in town the following week, it seemed the knocker was never still on the big front door. Cards and invitations poured in every day for a ball, a Venetian breakfast, an evening party at the theater, a riding expedition or a ridotto. Aunt Alice was ecstatic and declared that both she and Melissa must have some new clothes, for everyone had seen all their gowns, time out of mind! Uncle Ferdie did not argue, in fact he assured them that he expected his lovely ladies to outshine everyone else, and hang the expense! Melissa felt she barely had time to write an occasional letter to Wardley or to Rob, so busy as she was. There was for example Lady Warner's masked ball to prepare for, and for weeks before all society seemed to talk of nothing else. Several of Aunt Alice's friends called for the express purpose of discussing it, for it appeared that it was to be the event of the season.

Lady Warner's eldest son William, new back from India, was to be the guest of honor, and the quality who had seen nothing of the young man for several years were agog with excitement. There were rumors that he had made a tremendous fortune, and several ladies who were intimate with Lady Warner made the most of their privileged positions by describing the beautiful jewels and artifacts he had brought back from that country. Aunt Alice was piqued that she had to get her information second-hand, and knew nothing about it. She decided that she and Melissa would have their gowns made from Indian material and was delighted to find just what she had in mind in an exclusive warehouse specializing in imports.

She took the filmy silk saris to her favorite modiste, and Mme Thérèse was delighted with the beautiful stuff. Melissa's was a pale yellow, delicately embroidered all over in gold thread with peacocks and exotic flowers. Lady Throckmorton had chosen a deep blue silk edged in silver and declared herself pleased when she saw the results.

"For, my love," she confided as they were leaving the dressmaker's one afternoon after a fitting, "we are sure to make every other woman at the ball look insipid in comparison! I wonder—do you think diamonds or my sapphires would look best with my gown?"

Melissa voted firmly for the sapphires, knowing her aunt would probably try to wear both sets at once. The new dresser did not have a firm hand with her ladyship.

Aunt Alice had also obtained a voucher for Almack's, that most exclusive of clubs, and as soon as some of her new dresses were ready, insisted Ferdie escort them to what all society called "The Marriage Mart." Melissa saw several of the house party there, but the duke failed to put in an appearance. She danced one evening with Alan Cranston who let slip that Colchester had been called away from town on estate business. Melissa stifled an errant pang of regret by firmly telling herself she was delighted to have him out of the way.

Aunt Alice did not seem to be the type who frequented Almack's very often, and she made no secret of her reasons for doing so now. On their very first visit, when she came to inspect Melissa's new white gown and pale pink accessories, she told her in no uncertain terms the object of their attendance.

"You will of course, dear Melissa, realize that although Mr. Whitney did not come up to scratch, there are many other fish for the catching! However, this season is your one and only chance, and I expect you to make the most of the opportunity your Uncle Ferdie and I provide. Almack's is excessively boring to *me,* you know! Oh, one last thought! You are on no account to waltz until one of the patronesses gives you permission! That would be too bold, destroy all our chances! Be maidenly and modest—la, how can you help it, dressed like that? I wonder if I was a little too obvious with all the pink?"

It did not appear that this was the case, however, for when they entered the rooms, Melissa's card was quickly filled and the evening passed smoothly. Aunt Alice was pleased when Lady Jersey had a smile for her niece, although Countess Esterhazy, who had always disapproved of Lady Throckmorton, turned her back on the three of them with a frown.

Melissa was surprised to see Mr. Whitney there, carefully in attendance on an imposing dowager in purple. She sat solidly on a small sofa against the wall, her purple plumes waving regally above her turban as she inspected all the young ladies carefully. Mr. Whitney saw Melissa and bent to speak to his mother. She raised her quizzing glass and subjected Melissa to a prolonged stare. Melissa had the oddest desire to do something truly outrageous, but she controlled herself and pretended not to notice them.

Mr. Whitney nodded faintly to her once when they met in the same set. She lowered her eyes demurely, while noting with amusement that he was dancing with quite the thinnest, palest, most demure debutante present. Had Mrs. Whitney chosen her as worthy of her dear Chauncy, she wondered?

The evening of the Warner ball at last arrived. In addition to the lovely yellow sari, Aunt Alice had Melissa's hair dressed in the very plain style favored by Indian ladies. It was parted in the middle, brushed smooth, and then drawn back severely into a large coil, low on her neck. Many girls would have found it difficult to carry off, but it seemed to add mystery to Melissa's face beneath the half mask of yellow silk.

As the Throckmortons ascended the stairs to greet their hostess, Melissa drew many eyes, but none so intent as Lord Warner's. He seemed almost startled as she curtsied to his mother and to him, and it was not long before he sought her out in the crowded ballroom to beg her for a dance. Melissa thought she had seldom seen such a handsome man! He was tall and deeply tanned, and his blond hair was bleached almost white from the tropic sun. He wore no costume or mask, and his evening dress was impeccable. When he smiled down at her, Melissa felt an answering stir inside her.

"I have been away too long, I fear, Miss Ward!" he remarked. "When I saw you coming up the stairs, I could have sworn we had met before, a very long way from England! And yet, now I realize that you are much too fair to be a native of India! Where had you the sari? It is most faithful to the materials I have seen abroad."

Melissa explained her aunt's wish to honor him by wearing native dress, and he thanked her. "I look forward to the unmasking at midnight!" he said, bowing to her as the dance ended. "Do you have melting brown eyes behind that intriguing mask?"

Melissa felt suddenly very sorry for her bright blue eyes, but she only smiled and allowed him to take her back to her aunt.

She had no dearth of partners, and the evening passed quickly, even though Lord Warner did not approach her again. She often felt his eyes on her, however, and in response, a surge of happiness. At midnight, the orchestra sounded a fanfare, and amidst much laughing and jest, the guests unmasked. Melissa's partner, struggling with his own mask, could not help her untangle the strings of hers, and suddenly she heard a soft voice behind her say, "Allow me to assist you, Miss Ward!" She turned breathlessly and smiled up at Lord Warner, her eyes widening as she saw the faint look of disappointment on his face which he quickly concealed by bowing over her hand.

"Of course, I might have known!" he said jestingly, tucking her hand in his and preparing to lead her to the supper room. "An English rose after all, with eyes the color of the English sky!" He was so fervent, Melissa felt she must have misinterpreted his first reaction. They chatted easily throughout supper, and when Lord Warner asked her if he might call, she was happy to assure him she would be delighted.

All the way home, Aunt Alice raved about the young lord—his blond good looks, his polished manners, and not least of all, the fortune he had acquired during his years abroad. When Melissa told her he was coming to call, she was ecstatic. "How wonderful, dear Melissa! Thank heavens Chauncy Whitney drew back after all!" As her aunt continued to enthuse,

Melissa wanted to restrain her for a morning call, after all, was not a proposal of marriage! She herself, although she had been attracted to Lord Warner, still felt a pang of uneasiness when she recalled his face at the unmasking. He had been attentive and charming thereafter, but had there not been in his demeanor a slight coldness and withdrawal? She had the sudden thought that perhaps she was merely comparing him to the Duke of Colchester, and no one could accuse him of coldness! That must be it; she was so used to the duke's flashing dark eyes and impetuous advances that she was unused to the behavior of a real gentleman!

True to his word, Lord Warner arrived in the morning, with a bouquet of flowers for each of the ladies. He stayed the conventional fifteen minutes and then took his leave, but not before ascertaining that the Throckmortons planned to attend Almack's that evening.

It was not long before all the quality were buzzing about Melissa and the newly returned heir. Her other beaux still clustered around, but it was Lord Warner who always seemed to be there to take her in to supper, or find her the best seat at a musicale, next to him of course, or fetch her a glass of claret punch at a dance. One evening he and his mother invited Melissa and the Throckmortons to the theater, where their box attracted many eyes. Melissa knew Lord Warner admired her, but she was confused. In spite of his constant attentions, there was none of the lover in his eyes when he smiled at her, and although he spoke freely and easily of his years abroad, she felt he was only telling a very little of what was really in his mind. By this time she had seen too many young men blush and stammer when

they approached her not to recognize the symptoms
of a man who fancied himself in love, and although
Lord Warner behaved like a serious suitor, he
remained cool, considerate and polite. It was a puz-
zle!

When the Duke of Colchester arrived in town, he
was quickly made aware of Melissa's newest conquest. Percy Marshall told him as the two friends
strolled to Brooks's for an evening's play. "The *on-dit*
of the season, my dear Tony! He had barely unpacked
his trunks before he fell head over heels in love, or so
the gossips have it!" Lord Marshall stole a glance at
his friend's frowning face and smiled. "You do not
look a bit pleased; now why is that, I wonder? Did
you think the one stage kiss you stole would make
the lady forever immune to others?"

Tony replied wryly, "Not at all, my dear, not at
all! Miss Ward has all too often given me the set-
down royal for me to have any conceit left! Besides, I
have it from my Aunt Reagen that he is a young god,
Adonis himself come amongst us, bearing bags of
money! How could any female resist the combina-
tion?"

Lord Marshall thought the duke sounded singularly
bitter, so he deftly changed the subject.

The duke had a chance to observe the couple for
himself the following evening when he attended a
ball given by the Earl and Countess of Wythe. As he
entered the ballroom, there right in front of him
waltzing gaily was Melissa Ward, beautiful in palest
peach silk, and in the arms of a handsome man so
tanned it had to be Lord Warner. He bent and
whispered something in her ear, and she smiled up
at him charmingly. The duke made his way leisurely to Lady Throckmorton's side and without

even having to ask, was made privy to all that lady's hopes concerning her niece and the catch of the year. Lady Throckmorton was thrilled for more than one reason. Of course it was a pleasant plum for her if Melissa married well, but there was more to it than that. She was becoming extremely tired of having Melissa with her. Vain as she was, even she knew that side by side she looked old compared to Melissa's fresh, young beauty. If only the chit would marry, she often thought, I would be free of her! And surely I have been most generous with my time and efforts, saddled as I am with a young girl in her first season. It became tiresome!

When the dance ended, Lord Warner returned Melissa to her aunt and was introduced to the duke. They exchanged a few courteous words, and then Lord Warner withdrew as Melissa's next partner arrived. The duke thought him cold, and wondered what a hothead like Melissa could see in him? He will bore her in a month, even with those good looks and all the money, he thought cynically, but he was surprised to find he was more than a little perturbed by the prospect of their marriage. He put his feelings down to the wager he had with Melissa—this was no Chauncy Whitney he had to deal with now! He did not try for a dance with the lady, however, and after a little while took his leave of his hostess and left the ball. Melissa watched him go thoughtfully. While he had been talking with Lord Warner she had studied them both carefully and was pleased to find that Lord Warner came out ahead in all her comparisons. The duke was a rake; Lord Warner was a perfect gentleman. One was impetuous; the other, careful and considerate. How could any girl prefer that dark, arrogant face to such sunny good looks? And

Lord Warner did not frighten her; he had never so
much as pressed her hand too fervently, and he had
certainly never tried to kiss her! Melissa sighed.
Yes, a perfect gentleman, even on that evening at
Vauxhall when they had become separated from the
rest of their party, he had been all that was correct.
Why then did she feel such regret when the duke left
so abruptly, without even asking her for a dance?
She went to bed that night in a state of confusion.

The next morning when the post had been delivered,
her maid brought her a letter from Rob. Melissa was
in her room preparing to dress for a morning's shopping with Aunt Alice, but she sank down on a velvet
chair near the window and opened it happily. It had
been such a long time since Rob had written! But
when she had finished the letter, her eyes were wide
with horror and concern, and she crushed the pages
in her hands absently. Rob confessed that he had
played deep, the last few days of the Christmas
house party, and had lost a great deal of money. He
had been so sure his luck would change that he
continued to gamble, plunging deeper and deeper.
His opponents, two young sprigs of fashion who had
more money than was good for them, had assumed
young Rob was also plump in the pockets. They
parted from him assuring him they were in no hurry
to be paid; next quarter day would be fine should he
find himself strapped and with pockets to let. He had
gone back to school in desperation. He could not find
it in himself to confess to Uncle Ferdie, and the
thought of begging Aunt Alice to assist him was too
much, even for him. At last, he wrote his sister, and
in laying the burden on her shoulders, immediately
felt a great deal better. Lissa would contrive! Let her
call on Mr. Bentley in town and all would be well!

Melissa was stunned. She smoothed out the pages and read the fatal amount again. No, she had not been mistaken. Five hundred pounds! She knew without looking that she had only some twenty guineas to her name, and even more than Rob she could not bear to burden her uncle further after he had been so kind and generous to her. She asked her maid to make her excuses to Lady Throckmorton, saying she had a slight headache and wished to rest.

After the maid left, she paced up and down her bedroom for a long time, wondering what to do. In her mind's eye, a long moon-lit road stretched before her, a coach thundering along it, while in a dark wood she waited on Captain, pistols cocked and drawn, and she shuddered. Not that way, not ever again! If only the wager were won, she would have plenty, but three months remained before she could expect the duke to pay his debt. Rob could not wait that long; gentlemen of honor paid their debts promptly if they did not wish to get an unsavory reputation. Melissa sighed. There was no way out but to call on Mr. Bentley. She did not know his direction, but surely the butler would be able to help her, even if he felt it a bit unusual for a young girl to seek her solicitor alone. She summoned her maid and dressed in the plainest walking dress she owned, and donned a matching straw bonnet. As she drew on her gloves and picked up her reticule, she wished, with a flash of temper, that she had Rob before her now. What a set-down she would have given him!

As she came down the stairs, the butler was ushering the Duke of Colchester into the hall.

"My dear Miss Ward, well met!" he exclaimed cheerfully, his countenance lighting up in a grin. "I was just coming to ask you if you would care to go for

a drive this morning? It is a perfect day for a tour of
the park, and since I am informed that your aunt
has gone out, you must allow me to amuse you!"

Melissa tried not to frown. If her mind had not
been so preoccupied with Rob's problem, she might
have thought quickly of an excuse, but she seemed
to be numb. The last person she wanted to see was
the duke, but like a bad penny, here he was! He took
her hand and, tucking it under his arm, said airily to
the Throckmorton butler, "Be so kind as to inform
her ladyship that Miss Ward is with me, and I shall
take the greatest care of her!"

Melissa found herself walked calmly to the door,
and was aware that unless she was prepared to
make a scene, she was committed to a morning with
the duke. She tried to draw back, but his hand closed
over hers tightly, as the butler bowed and held the
front door for them. The duke helped her into his
phaeton and whispered, "At last! Providence is surely
on my side this lovely morning, dear Lissa!" Mounting
the step and taking up the reins, he motioned to his
tiger to let them go. Melissa was relieved when the
tiger jumped up behind.

Melissa sat as far from the duke as she could, to
his infinite amusement, her back straight and her
chin high. He chatted away amiably, ignoring her
silence, and when they had maneuvered the tricky
gates at the park entrance, he gave his team the
office to go. They were soon tooling rapidly down the
road. It *is* a beautiful morning, Melissa thought
sadly, if only I had the spirit to enjoy it! The sun
shone warmly, promising a not-too-distant summer,
the sky was bright blue, and there was only the
gentlest of breezes.

They had covered most of the park, nodding to all

the other riders who were enjoying the day, when the duke suddenly halted his team and ordered the tiger to their heads. He jumped lightly to the ground and came around to Melissa's side. Imperiously holding out his hand, he ordered, "Come! It is much too find a day to forego a stroll through the gardens! The daffodils are displaying beautifully; you would not care to miss them!"

Melissa looked around desperately and saw Lady Jersey driving towards them, a gay smile on her face for the duke, and knew she had no choice. If she could not make a scene in front of the Throckmorton butler, even less could she do so before Lady Jersey and her party. She shrugged and accepted his hand.

As they walked through the gravel paths around the lake, the duke continued to chat until they were out of sight of the main drive. "What can be the matter, dear Lissa? Not a word have you honored me with this morning, not even an insult or a set-down! Come," he added, a note of asperity in his voice, "even if I am not the handsome Lord Nabob, you might at least make an effort to appear reasonably content!" He drew her down to a stone seat facing the lake and took both her hands in his. "Dearest Lissa! Do smile for me or I shall be forced to kiss away your abstraction!" He moved to take her in his arms, and she pushed him away abruptly.

"Oh, stop! I have no time for such foolishness now!"

The duke's eyebrows rose alarmingly, and his arms dropped.

"Foolishness? Can I have heard you correctly? But how do you expect me to win our wager if I am not allowed an occasional kiss? And you are quite, quite alone with me here. I can, and will have it, you know!"

Melissa waved him away impatiently. "I wish you would not be so silly, Your Grace! I have no time to think of you today!"

For a moment the duke appeared stunned. It was surely the first time in his long career as lover that he had been so thoroughly repulsed, and in such a way too! The lady had "no time" for him; she had told him he was "foolish" and "silly"! Adjectives such as these had never come his way, and it so bemused him that he dropped the pose of lover and became serious.

"What is the matter, Miss Ward?" he asked formally. "If there is any way that I can be of service, I should be glad to assist you!"

Melissa stared at him and shook her head, her face white and set. "I thank you for your kindness, sir," she began just as formally, but he interrupted her quickly.

"Enough! There *is* something wrong! Now what can it be? Is Lady Throckmorton bothering you? Or perhaps there is trouble at home? 'Tis not your little sister, or that handsome younger brother, is it?" His eyes narrowed as he saw her start involuntarily and twist the strings of her reticule, and he leaned back and folded his arms.

"Aha! 'Tis Master Rob! No, do not tell me, let me guess!" he said, raising a hand, although Melissa had made no move to speak. "The cub has been sent down from school? No? He has fallen madly in love with a most unsuitable older woman? No? Let me think!" He stared across the lake while Melissa studied her smart kid slippers.

"I believe I have the scenario now! Master Rob

finds himself deeply in debt; in fact he probably fell into it during the house party at Beechwoods, did he not? And since he isn't man enough to own up to it to his uncle, and had the decency not to go to his aunt—(be thankful for small favors, Lissa!)—he has written to you and asked you to get him out of his predicament. You probably received the letter this morning, and that is why you are so distraught. Come, my girl, out with it! What is the horrible sum?"

Melissa stared at him. "But . . . but how did you know?" she asked wonderingly.

The duke laughed. "One meeting with your brother was all I needed to take his measure, and I did observe him more than once in the company of young Ashton-Lowry and Lord Beekins. Silly fools both, but they are so well-to-do it matters not whether they win or lose! Come, tell me the amount!"

Melissa rose and paced up and down, and when the duke joined her and took her arm, she looked up at him pleadingly. "I cannot, Your Grace! It is not your concern, and should be handled only by a member of the Ward family. I was on my way to our solicitor when I met you in the hall. He will know what to do!"

Colchester led her back to the carriage. "Oh, that would be White, would it not? Good man!"

"No," Lissa said absently, "Papa always used George Bentley."

The duke stored the name away, and did not refer to the matter again. Instead, as he handed her into her seat in the phaeton, he grinned up at her and said, "I knew it had to be a very serious problem, dear Lissa! Nothing else could account for your being able to resist my charms so thoroughly!"

Melissa bridled. "Conceited man!" she hissed at him, and he laughed. He drove her sedately back to the Throckmorton town house, and as he took his leave of her at the front door, advised her to put Master Rob's problems from her mind for a few days.

"Sometimes it is better to wait, rather than to act in the heat of the moment. What a shame the wager still has some time to run! You would be well above in the world then! But remember," he added wickedly, "I have three months, and I still intend to make you fall in love with me!"

Melissa gave him her hand and said haughtily, "I bid you good day sir! What a very great pity that you will discover that your charms are not so . . . not so *overwhelming* as you believe!"

The duke removed his hat and bowed elegantly, laughing as he did so. "Three months, dear Lissa! That is plenty of time! And bear in mind, my dear, the Northrups never give up!"

There was such a serious glint to his dark eyes, and such a determined set to that sensuous mouth, that Melissa only nodded distantly and quickly entered the house. It was too late to seek out Mr. Bentley now, for Aunt Alice would soon be home, and they had promised to drink tea with Mrs. Hodges, an old friend of Lady Alice's. Melissa did ask the butler to find out Mr. Bentley's direction, and if that staid and serious servant wondered why the young lady did not ask her solicitor to call on her, he made no mention of it as he assured her he would do so without delay.

For some reason, Melissa felt better than she had before driving out with the duke, and although the problem of Rob's debt still remained, she went up to change her gown cheerfully. She had been surprised when the duke, who had her completely alone, had so suddenly dropped his amorous pose and seriously offered to help her. But of course that was impossible. She must not fall into his debt, of all people! Perhaps that was why he offered, she thought cynically, so that she would look more kindly on him! Never would she let him help her, not in this or in anything!

Besides, this was Ward business, and a Ward would settle it. She determined to call on Mr. Bentley in the morning.

CHAPTER 11

Melissa's Ball; The Right Proposal

It was, however, three days before Melissa had a morning free and was able to take a hack, accompanied by her maid, to Mr. Bentley's office in Tudor Street. A very young clerk with inky fingers and a green eyeshade got down from his high stool to admit them, and went to tell the lawyer of her arrival.

Mr. Bentley himself came out of his room to greet her and led her to a seat, after asking her maid to wait outside. Melissa poured out her troubles, sparing Rob nothing. She was amazed that the elderly lawyer took the news so calmly, and he rose in her estimation because of it. When she finished and asked him what they were to do, he said he would send the money immediately to Rob, along with a stern letter of warning to watch what he was about. He also asked her to do her best to inform her brother that the estate could stand no more of his profligacy, and if he were not more prudent in the future, Wardley Hall would have to be sold. Mr. Bentley did not mention the visit to his office of a very important personage, some three afternoons previously, nor did he embarrass the young lady by congratulating her on her wealthy benefactor. Discreetness was his watchword! Besides, he was well aware that if Miss Ward could not fancy the Duke of Colchester, there was a Lord Warner waiting in the wings. He rubbed his hands gleefully after he bowed the lady out. Things were definitely looking up for the Ward fortunes, if only that young scamp did not land them all in debtors' prison before his sister was secured to a man of wealth! He looked forward to arranging the generous marriage settlements he would insist on from whomever the lady finally decided to favor.

Melissa went immediately to her desk when she returned home and wrote a scathing letter to her brother. They had been fortunate this time, but there must be no more repetitions of such wildness! She hoped Rob had been frightened enough to heed her and Mr. Bentley, and when she dressed that evening to go out, she felt happier than she had in days.

She continued to see Lord Warner almost every day, and it seemed that whenever they were together, she would look up at one point or another to find the Duke of Colchester cynically observing them. Several times she had the feeling that Lord Warner was on the point of proposing, but he always drew back and made no move to seek an interview with her uncle. It confused her. If he did speak, what would be her answer? At times, she felt she would say yes gladly; at others she felt a vague uneasiness and a premonition that her answer would be no, and for no reason that made a particle of sense to her.

Besides all her regular activities and the daily rides in the park with her uncle, an exercise that neither of them wished to give up whatever the circumstances, she was also extremely busy helping her aunt prepare for an elaborate ball. Although no one mentioned it, she knew that it was to be held in her honor, and that Aunt Alice was hoping and praying that the ball might tip the odds in favor of a proposal from Lord Warner, and that she might have a happy announcement to make shortly thereafter.

It made a great deal of work which fell to Melissa and the servants. The invitations had to be written and delivered, the orchestra hired, the extra help approved by the butler, china and crystal augmented, and special delicacies ordered from London's finest caterer to assist the already overworked chef and his kitchen staff. Aunt Alice approved the flowers Melissa ordered, and even spent a morning in the ballroom overseeing the hanging of the pink silk she had decided must drape the walls. Melissa and the staff held their breaths until she declared herself satisfied, and took herself off to a loo party.

Melissa was to wear a new gown of white brocade with white roses in her hair, and there were innumerable fittings before Lady Throckmorton was satisfied with the effect.

The morning of the ball dawned clear and warm, almost unseasonably so for late spring. Melissa and her uncle were up early to ride in the park, and they saw no one but a few grooms exercising the horses of the quality who chose to remain in bed. As they rode, Uncle Ferdie declared they must have lanterns in the garden that adjoined the ballroom, in case the guests cared to stroll about between the sets, and took himself off as soon as they reached the house to see to the arrangements. As Melissa entered the hall, everything was in a great bustle. Furniture was being moved and flowers delivered, and several footmen were engaged in polishing the prisms of the large chandelier in the front hall. Melissa was surprised to see the number of floral tributes that had arrived for her, as many as there were for Lady Throckmorton! She hoped that that lady would have at least one more bouquet than she received herself, for the sake of peace! Lord Warner had sent white roses—had Aunt Alice given him the hint, Melissa wondered? From the Duke of Colchester there was a bouquet of many beautiful and strange flowers from one of his succession houses. Their fragrance was especially sensuous, and Melissa realized that in their natural environment, these flowers would grow profusely in a jungle; hot, moist and wild. It disturbed her, and she placed the bouquet to the back of the table in the hall where the offerings were to be displayed. It was not difficult to hide it for Lord Marshall, Alan Cranston and several of her other admirers had also honored her.

As she was being dressed in the white brocade after her hair had been elaborately arranged, taking what seemed like hours to an impatient young lady on the eve of her very own ball, her aunt arrived. Melissa turned slowly, this way and that, displaying the white rosebuds in her hair; her mother's pearls, her long white kid gloves, and the shining white satin slippers that all complimented the stiff fabric of the brocade. The gown had been cut to cling to her figure well below the waist before it belled out gracefully. Lady Throckmorton, resplendent in the deep rose she had chosen to coordinate with the pink silk hangings of the ballroom, was pleased.

"Perfection, Melissa! You are everything I hoped, and if *this* does not win the trick, I do not know what will!" She rose to leave, gathering her gown in one bejeweled hand. At the door she turned and said imperiously, "You will carry Lord Warner's roses, of course! If he had sent roadside wildflowers you would still have carried them! Do I make myself clear?"

The two women looked at each other, Lady Throckmorton seriously determined; Melissa uncertain and confused. It was Melissa who lowered her eyes first, and blushed. Aunt Alice had pinned all her hopes on this evening, and she was making it extremely plain what she expected of her niece. It was a warning, a warning that Melissa did not know how to answer. She was able to forget her aunt's haughty look of command when the guests began to arrive and were ushered to where the Throckmortons and the vision in white brocade were waiting to receive them at the door to the ballroom. As ordered, Melissa carried Lord Warner's white roses. The Duke of Colchester, bowing over her hand, saw them at once and raised a cynical brow. Melissa thought she had never seen him look so handsome as he did this evening in his immaculate evening dress, his white cravat a startling contrast to his dark face and black hair, one lock of which fell over his forehead as he bent over her hand.

"Ah, Lissa, how lovely!" he whispered. "But perhaps just a trifle ... hmm ... obvious, don't you think?" He smiled at her as she drew her hand away and turned to Lord Marshall who gracefully complimented her until she had to laugh with him.

Lord Warner also noticed his bouquet and thanked her for carrying it. He looked intently at her as he spoke, no hint of a smile on his lips or in his eyes. Melissa's heart beat strangely. Was this the face of a man about to declare his love? He looked rather as if he were seriously doubting his next move, or reconsidering it. Melissa assured him she would be delighted to give him the first waltz, and shyly welcomed his mother, who smiled happily at her and pressed her hand meaningfully. Lady Warner was definitely on the side of Lady Throckmorton! From their first meeting when her son had shown such interest in Melissa, she had always treated her with warmth and kindness and done all she could to promote the match. No Mrs. Whitney here!

Melissa opened the ball dancing with her uncle. He was so delighted with his niece and so happy for her that her spirits rose. She had learned to love this shy, inarticulate man who seemed so pleased to present her to society, and was so fond of her. Surely no daughter could have been as blessed as she was, and so she smiled at him and whispered, "Dear Uncle Ferdie! How can I ever thank you for this beautiful ball and everything you have done for me?"

Lord Throckmorton blushed and stammered, and grew so agitated by her praise that he missed his step. Melissa stopped trying to tell him what was in her heart. Tomorrow she would seek him out and thank him properly she decided.

She danced every dance. After his waltz Lord

Warner left her reluctantly to the Duke of Colchester. He had spoken of inconsequentialities as they danced, and there was nothing in his manner that showed that this evening was any different from any other ball they had attended together. The duke held her closely and murmured compliments in her ear until she blushed and tried to draw away. "Lissa, my love, are you blushing?" he asked wickedly, holding her even tighter. "Can it be that you are at last succumbing to the inevitable? You know you care for me! Come, admit it!" He kissed her hand warmly as the dance ended, and Melissa was glad to escape him without answering such outrageous statements.

The ballroom grew warm as the evening wore on, for the press of the huge number of guests, the many chandeliers with their blazing candles and the dancing made it seem almost summery. Soon many of the guests were strolling in the garden, fanning themselves. Lord Throckmorton beamed when his wife complimented him on his forethought, and gallantly took her for a turn so she might see the colored lanterns and the gilt chairs and tables he had ordered to be placed in any convenient nook.

When Lord Warner came to claim his second dance, Melissa was fanning herself with her dance card. Lord Marshall had just romped her through a vigorous country dance, and she was breathless. Lord Warner took her hand gravely, and observing her flushed cheeks and sparkling eyes, asked her if she would care to forego their dance and walk with him in the garden instead. Melissa was glad to agree. She had no desire to faint from the heat which suddenly seemed so oppressive.

They reached the terrace and made their way down the slope to the garden, Melissa nervously chatting about the ball, and wondering if she had made a mistake in allowing Lord Warner to take her out. He said nothing until they reached the fountain in the middle, and Melissa grew silent. There was no one else about, something she had not expected. Still without a word he seated her and then walked a few steps away, his back turned to her as he contemplated the tinkling water of the fountain. Melissa's eyes grew wide, and her heart began to pound. Suddenly he seemed to come to a decision, for he turned back and took the seat next to her.

"My dear Miss Ward!" he began, leaning towards her, his eyes earnest and intent on her face. "It must have come to your notice how highly I revere you!" He took her hand in both of his and pressed it to his heart. "I should not speak to you before I have your uncle's permission, but I must know . . . can it be possible that you return my esteem?"

Melissa stared at him breathlessly. Here was the proposal that Aunt Alice was waiting for, but why did he not smile? He looked as if he were asking her for the privilege of taking her in to supper! Before she could reply, a cold, angry voice spoke behind them.

"One hesitates to interrupt such a touching *tête-à-tête*, but Miss Ward is promised to me for the next dance!"

Lord Warner dropped her hand and rose. Melissa had the strange thought that he was relieved as he bowed to her and the duke and prepared to take his leave.

"I will call on your uncle and on you tomorrow, Miss Ward!" he said correctly, and left her sitting by the fountain in confusion with the duke staring down at her, anger in his eyes.

"Well, my girl," he said grimly, "it appears that I was just in time! Is it possible that you were actually considering his proposal of marriage seriously?" He strode up and down the path before her as he spoke, and suddenly whirled and pointed a finger at her accusingly. "You would be bored in a month! For all his Indian adventures, he is milk and water! You need a man, a strong virile man to satisfy you!"

He would have continued, but Melissa rose and said icily, "Like yourself, Your Grace? Thank you, but no thank you!"

The duke suddenly grinned. "Do consider what you say! I have not availed myself of the privilege of asking for your hand, my dear!"

She blushed scarlet and made to leave him, but he reached out a strong hand and pulled her to him, his eyes glinting strangely in the light of the lanterns.

"Oh, no, you don't! You do not just walk away from me; that would be too easy! It is much too warm to dance, so let us also enjoy the garden! Why should I be denied the boon you granted to Lord Warner so easily?" As he spoke, he pulled her into his arms, and Melissa fought him as hard as she could, speechless with anger. When he had her enclosed tightly in his arms with his powerful hands holding her close to him, he bent his head and stared into her eyes. She stared back, trying to convey her fury and indifference to his nearness although her heart was beating strangely. He continued to look deeply into her eyes for a long moment, and then he covered her lips with his own. Once again Melissa experienced the sensation of drowning she had felt on the stage at Beechwoods. If he does not stop I will be lost, she thought wildly! Slowly, lingeringly, the duke raised his head. Melissa's eyes filled with tears as she stared up at him in confusion. He was not smiling now; his face was stern and serious, his dark eyes intent on her face. For a long moment they remained frozen, and then, as one sparkling tear ran down her face, he sighed and released her. He took out his handkerchief and dried her eyes carefully before he tucked her hand in his arm and led her back to the ballroom without a word, his face serious with thought.

Melissa excused herself as soon as they reached the terrace and he made no move to stop her as she entered the ballroom alone and made her way hastily to her aunt's side. That lady looked at her searchingly, but there was no opportunity to question her for General Adams had arrived to take the chair at Lady Throckmorton's side. Melissa excused herself and left them gossiping together as she went to the small salon that had been set aside for the ladies withdrawing room to compose herself. She did not hear the chattering of the other ladies, or see the speculative looks that many of them gave her. Her disappearance from the ballroom with Lord Warner had not escaped notice, nor his reappearance alone, and when the more astute looked around, it could be seen that the Duke of Colchester was also *in absentia*. Society would ponder and gossip over this tidbit for many days! Melissa was not aware she had become an object of intense interest for she was considering what she would say to her aunt when she was questioned, and to Lord Warner when he called in the morning!

The ball was ruined for her from that point, although she continued dancing and conversing gaily with all her partners. She was glad Lord Marshall had nipped in ahead of Lord Warner and the duke for the privilege of taking her in to supper, and she tried hard to entertain him over the lobster patties and jellies and her uncle's excellent champagne. He noticed her agitation without appearing to do so, and talked gently and soothingly until she seemed more relaxed.

The ball was a great success so everyone declared as they left. Lady Throckmorton was pleased, Lord Throckmorton complacent, and Melissa confused as she went up to bed very late and tried to sleep. She was called to the drawing room the next morning before her aunt had a chance to summon her and find out what had happened, and found Lord Warner there with her uncle. Uncle Ferdie beamed at her and made his excuses to leave them alone. It was obvious that he considered the young man a perfect match for his niece and approved wholeheartedly.

Melissa accepted a nosegay of white rosebuds with nerveless hands and asked Lord Warner to be seated. She took a chair across from him and tried to smile as he considered her gravely.

"Melissa!" he began, setting down the glass of Madeira he had been drinking with Lord Throckmorton. "I have your permission to so address you?" She nodded faintly, never taking her eyes from his face.

"Your uncle has been kind enough to approve my suit. Now it only remains for you to tell me that I do not aspire to your hand in vain!"

Melissa considered him carefully before she answered. "M'lord! You honor me! But . . . but, I do not know what to say!"

She stopped in confusion and Lord Warner came and went down on one knee before her, looking up into her face earnestly.

"Why, my dear, you say 'thank you very much, I would be delighted!' Or perhaps, 'I am very sorry, m'lord, but we should not suit!' " He smiled faintly and added, "I would hope it would be the first sentiment of course!" He pressed her hand and rose, looking down at her as he awaited her answer.

Melissa got up in some agitation, and paced up and down, lost in thought. Finally she raised her head and looked at him directly.

"This is very difficult for me, m'lord, and you must forgive me that I ask, but . . . but . . . do you love me? I had not expected a proposal like this . . . and I am not sure what your feelings are towards me!" She stopped, confused, feeling she had been too bold as she saw his sudden frown. He came to her quickly and took her hand.

"I had hoped to avoid this," he muttered as if to himself, and then spoke slowly. "I have a great affection for you, Melissa, and a great esteem, but I do not love you."

Melissa tried to release her hand but he held it more tightly and said earnestly, "Wait! Please hear me! I am proposing a marriage of convenience of course. I must marry, my name demands it! The reason that I do not love you, the reason that I can never love you is because I am already in love, irrevocably and forever!" He groaned and put his hands over his eyes as Melissa stared at him in wonder.

"But, m'lord . . . if you are in love already, why do you ask *me* to marry you? Why do you not ask *her?*"

He raised his head and stared at her, and Melissa

thought she had never seen such naked suffering in anyone's face in her entire life.

"I cannot!" he said mournfully. "Come, sit down and I will tell you the whole." He led her to a sofa and sat down beside her. He began hesitatingly, but soon forgot to be self-conscious as he described the Indian princess he had met and fallen in love with during his years abroad. Melissa listened, lost in the story until he ended, "So you see, I cannot marry my princess, it is out of the question. I must marry an Englishwoman of good birth. Marriage to my beloved Ameera would never be accepted! You and I, Melissa, are of the quality and as such we are not free to marry where we choose. Forgive me if I hurt you, but I believe that you also could not give your heart as you might wish; I have heard of your circumstances, your family troubles. . . ." Melissa stiffened as he continued with his story. "So I gave up Ameera and returned home to take my father's place as head of the family. I knew it was my duty to choose my bride well. Believe me, my dear Melissa, you would never be unhappy! I would do everything in my power to see to your comfort and care. You would never want for anything; I have riches beyond imagining! Is it so difficult to accept the admiration and security I offer you?" He paused to await her reply. Melissa stared at his earnest, good-looking face in confusion. All the answers to her problems— and Wardley's—were here. She only had to agree to a marriage of convenience to a gentle man who would care for her for the rest of her life, and all her troubles would be resolved. Was that so hard? Lord Warner was a vast improvement over a Chauncy Whitney after all! But she could not, not even for

Wardley! Something deep inside herself rebelled. It was all very well to be wealthy and protected and honored, but by a man who every time he looked at her would be comparing her to his lost love? She rose, her mind made up.

When she would have spoken, Lord Warner interrupted her. "Perhaps I have been too precipitous! You may want time to consider my proposal, and I can certainly understand that! It might be better if I called again in a few days when you have had time to consider. . . ."

Melissa stood very straight, her face white. "I do not think it would make any difference, m'lord," she heard herself say. "I am afraid my answer must be the same then as it is now. I am honored by your proposal of course, but I cannot accept it!"

She stopped in confusion as he bowed his head, and she felt tears of remorse and sorrow for him rising in her eyes. She wished she could accept, for his sake! Impulsively she went to him and took his hands.

"Come, m'lord! You do not truly wish to marry if you cannot forget the woman you love! Perhaps in a few years you may feel differently, and the pain of it will fade and allow you to find someone you can love!"

He smiled at her sadly. "If it cannot be you, I do not know who could erase her memory, but thank you!" He bowed to her and prepared to leave.

"My offer still stands, Melissa!" he said. "I will not change my mind, I shall only hope that you can find it in your heart to change yours!"

She shook her head gently and went with him to the door. As the butler handed him his hat and gloves, she smiled sadly in farewell and went up the stairs to her room. She did not want to speak to anyone, not even her uncle who was probably waiting to hear from her, until she had ordered her tumbled thoughts. She certainly hoped for a few moments before her Aunt Alice summoned her and demanded to know the wedding date!

CHAPTER 12

Return to Wardley

To say that Lady Throckmorton was displeased was to understate the case in the extreme! When that lady woke and called her maid to bring her morning chocolate, she was surprised to find that her husband was seeking to speak to her immediately. Ferdie knew better; within the first week of their marriage he had been made to understand plainly that Lady Throckmorton expected to be left strictly alone until she had made her toilette and given permission for his attendance, and no deviations from this rule would be acceptable. It was with a frown that she permitted him to enter and seat himself next to her bed while she dismissed the maid and her dresser, but when she heard of Lord Warner's early visit and its purpose, she was all smiles.

"Ah, Ferdie, my love!" she exclaimed happily. "What a wonderful and happy occasion! I am so glad you came to me first to tell me! Let us send for dear,

dear Melissa and make our plans! What a fortunate girl she is, he is so rich, so handsome! What a coup for her . . . and for us!"

Lady Throckmorton did not even take the time to dress, but sent her maid to fetch Melissa whose heart sank at the summons. She nervously straightened her dress and hair, and then, putting up her chin, went to her aunt's bedchamber. When she saw her uncle was also to be present, she was dismayed, for she hated to disappoint him especially. Aunt Alice was wreathed in smiles and beckoned her niece to the bed for an embrace.

"Your uncle has been telling me the good news, my love," she began, but Melissa paused near the foot of the bed and took a deep breath.

"I am afraid you will not consider it good news, Aunt. I have refused Lord Warner."

Lady Throckmorton fell back against her pillows, her hand to her heart.

"Can I have heard you correctly, miss? *Refused Lord Warner?*" she screamed. "Oh, the ingratitude of it, after all our work and attentions! Why? Tell me why immediately!"

Melissa stole a glance at her uncle's stunned face and said, "I could not accept him for he does not love me. He proposed a marriage of convenience!" She lowered her eyes and blushed.

"And what of that, may I ask?" Lady Throckmorton said dangerously, throwing out her hands. "You are in no position to be so nice in your requirements, miss! Do you think your uncle and I are prepared to put up with you indefinitely. . . ?"

"Oh, I say Alice . . ." Lord Throckmorton began feebly, but she turned on him and hissed,

"Be quiet! If she is too proud to agree to such a

wonderful match I wash my hands of her! And so shall you, Ferdie, so shall you!"

Lord Throckmorton subsided, looking in anguish to Melissa.

"I understand, Aunt Alice," she said with dignity. "You have both been very kind to me, and I am sorry to disappoint you, but I cannot—I will not—marry Lord Warner!"

Lady Throckmorton sat bolt upright in bed and pointed her finger at her niece imperiously. "Then you must leave London as soon as your bags have been packed! You may not remain in *my* house under *my* wing for the remainder of the season, nor shall you come with us to Brighton as we had planned! Think well, my girl! This is your last chance to save both Wardley and yourself!"

Melissa bowed her head and twisted her hands together. "I understand, Aunt, but no amount of thinking will change my mind." She curtsied gravely. "I will have my maid begin packing immediately!"

Lord Throckmorton made to rise and go to his niece, but Lady Throckmorton shrieked and fell back on her pillows, declaring that such willfulness and base ingratitude had given her a spell. While he was searching for her salts and vinaigrette, Melissa made her escape.

"Get out of my sight, you ungrateful wretch! I never want to see you again!" Aunt Alice screamed after her, so upsetting a very small tweeny who was busy scrubbing the stairs, that she overturned her bucket of suds and burst into tears.

Melissa dashed a few angry tears from her eyes as she entered her room and shut the door. Why had she even expected that Uncle Ferdie would have

been able to help her, or that he would have understood her position? She had thought he might come
to her defense because he loved her. But she knew
now that Lady Throckmorton would never stand for
it and he was powerless to stand up to her. It was
several minutes before she was able to compose
herself and call her maid to begin the packing.

In the early afternoon after she had refused to go
down to luncheon, she received a message from Lord
Throckmorton crying off from their afternoon ride,
and was not surprised. What could he say that could
undo her aunt's hateful words? He asked her to let
him know when she planned to leave so he could
have the carriage made ready for her. Captain would
be ridden home by one of the outriders. Looking
around at the disorder, she realized it would be
better to start fresh in the morning, for she still had
to decide which gowns she was taking with her. The
beautiful clothes her uncle had bought for her were
in no way suitable for the country and she did not
feel she had the right to take them, but some things
she must have. The maid was folding the black habit
and a few of the more serviceable gowns, but there
were still many things to be selected or discarded.

She wrote Lord Throckmorton a short note, asking
for the carriage early the next day, and thanking
him for being so kind as to provide it, and then she
turned her attention back to the packing. Lady
Throckmorton decreed a tray for Melissa in her
room that evening. As she ate with little appetite,
she wondered whether society would be surprised
that she did not attend the theater with her aunt
and uncle that evening, after the triumph of the
ball.

By nine o'clock the next morning she was dressed

and ready, and she descended the stairs to find her uncle waiting for her in the hall. He drew her into a small morning room and took her in his arms without a word. Melissa had a lump in her throat, and when she saw the misery in his eyes, all her anger and disappointment at her uncle disappeared.

"It is all right, Uncle Ferdie! Really! Do not feel sorry for me for I am sure I will be happier back home. I fear I was never cut out to be a London lady after all!"

She kissed him warmly and let him take her out to the carriage and make sure she was comfortable. As the carriage pulled away, she looked back at him standing forlornly at the bottom of the steps and knew she had made the right choice. Lord Throckmorton might never admit it, but he was burdened with just the same kind of loveless marriage that Melissa had refused! She could never have been content to live in such a way! The maid Lord Throckmorton had sent with her peeped at the lady carefully, but there were no tears or sighs. Instead, she sat up straighter and looked at the countryside with interest, the further they got from town.

Aunt Cardell was surprised to find Melissa on the doorstep that afternoon, and looked her over shrewdly. Melissa smiled and laughed as she kissed her aunt and drew her into the library.

"Yes, yes, I know! You did not expect to see me here at the height of the season, did you, dear Aunt? I will tell you the whole—but stay! Where is Nancy?"

Mrs. Cardell told her Nancy was visiting at Blackwood, and Melissa took off her cloak and sank down on a shabby chair gratefully. "Then we will be quite alone! I have been sent home in disgrace, Aunt, because I refused a marriage of convenience!"

Her aunt would have spoken, but Melissa hurried on, anxious to get her confession over with. "Oh, yes, it would have been a great match! He is young, handsome and rich! Aunt Alice was in raptures! But he confessed he did not, could not love me ever, for he was already in love with a very unsuitable lady!" The tale was soon told, and her aunt assured her she had done the right thing.

"I am not so sure, Aunt," Melissa said sadly. "It would have meant that Wardley and all of us would be safe. It seems selfish of me for I did feel kindly towards him! It was just watching Uncle Ferdie's life with a woman who has never loved him that made me decide I could never go through with it! But what will we do now?"

Aunt Cardell refused to discuss it until morning when Melissa would be rested. She put her arm around her fashionable niece, and led her from the library. "Come, my dear, enough of this gloom! We are so glad to have you home, and Nancy will be in raptures, she has missed you so much! Time enough to worry about the future tomorrow!"

Melissa was glad to follow her advice, and wandered around her old home getting acquainted with it again. In spite of Lord Throckmorton's assistance, it did not look at all different, and Melissa was dismayed to find she was a little ashamed of it, so rundown and shabby, compared to her uncle's magnificent homes. It was a side of her nature she had never suspected, and she was glad she had left London when she did, or she might have become inured to the good things she had always loved, and come to consider wealth and show to be the most important part of life.

She went to bed in her old room that night after planning a morning ride on Captain, feeling much more comfortable and at ease than she had in a long time. Perhaps she might see Jack on the morrow! As she drifted off, she wondered what the duke would make of her sudden disappearance, and what excuses Aunt Alice might have given to Lord Warner and the rest of the quality. Knowing her aunt, she was sure she would be painted in all the most unflattering colors as an ungrateful, willful miss, and decided that she cared not a jot!

The early summer days passed quickly, and Melissa slipped easily back into Wardley's routine. There had been no communication with the Throckmortons, but she had received a letter from Lord Warner saying how sorry he was she had had to return to her home because of her Aunt Cardell's illness. Trust Aunt Alice, she thought impatiently, to leave the door ajar! He restated his desire to marry her, and said he would wait to hear from her. So far she had not had the heart to reply.

Jack was making plans to go up to London. He seemed stunned that his father had suggested it so suddenly, but Melissa was not at all surprised for she had seen the look on Mrs. Holland's face when she went over to call on the lady. In her fashionable gown and French bonnet, with her hair arranged to perfection, she was not the old Melissa Ward, best friend and crony to Jack Holland, but a force to be reckoned with. The good lady lost no time pointing this out to the squire who had a chance to observe it himself when Aunt Cardell and Melissa were invited to dinner. Dear Melissa has grown up he decided, and perhaps his wife was right, and Jack would forget his old playmate in favor of this stunning young woman in her low-cut gown who had learned how to converse and flirt so charmingly!

There were times when Melissa found herself impatient with life in the country. She had never realized how slow it was, or how boring, and one evening she felt like screaming at her dear aunt for discussing the possibility of rain the following day, for what must have been the twentieth time since luncheon. What difference did it make if they went to Washburn that day or the next? They were only going to purchase some plain cotton to repair the worn sheets! She chided herself when she experienced such ignoble thoughts, telling herself firmly that London had spoiled her, and she was no better than Lady Throckmorton, always wanting to be petted and amused.

Since her year of mourning was over, she was invited to many a picnic or small dancing party, but even these treats did not make her spirits lighten. The young gentlemen of the neighborhood tried hard to hold her attention—invariably she compared them with Lord Warner or the Duke of Colchester, and turned away. She rode Captain often and hard, for only when she was exhausted could she sleep well. Her Aunt Cardell watched her anxiously. There was something wrong, besides her refusal to marry for convenience, but what could it be that was troubling her niece?

Jack rode away to London, and his mother's sighs of relief at his escape from temptation were obvious to everyone but him, and then Melissa found herself even more alone. She attended church faithfully with Nancy and her aunt; she helped in the stillroom and with the mending just as she had always done; and she spent hours in the stables talking to Simon who was delighted to have Captain under his wing again. Melissa had solved the problem of his reappearance by informing the squire that her uncle had purchased him at Tattersall's for her, after she had described her favorite horse, with no idea he had been used for nefarious purposes and wasn't it a marvelous coincidence? What the squire thought of such a Banbury tale he kept to himself, but since the Young Gentleman was heard of no more in his district, he cared very little what had become of him. Melissa, placidly floating through the days in the quiet of the country sometimes found herself thinking longingly of her adventures on the high toby. At least it had not been boring! Rather than daydream, she quickly sought out her sister or her aunt and chatted determinedly of other things.

Rob came home for the summer holidays, just after a letter arrived from Lady Throckmorton. It was addressed to Mrs. Cardell and begged the indulgence of a visit from Nancy and Rob now that the Throckmortons had removed from London and were summering at Brighton. She gave their direction, assured dear Mrs. Cardell that Lord Throckmorton would be delighted to send his coach for the young people any day they specified, but mention of Melissa there was none. Reading the letter over, Melissa felt that to her Aunt Alice she was no more, just as if she had sailed away from England and vanished forever. It made her shiver.

Nancy was wild with excitement, for at fourteen she was growing up and considered herself quite the young lady. She besieged Melissa with questions about how she should behave, what she should wear, and Aunt Cardell swore she was wearing a rut in the road between Wardley Hall and Blackwood since she felt the need to discuss every new idea with her friend, Joan, as soon as one occurred to her.

Rob made no mention of the payment of his debt, which astounded Melissa. She had thought that he might have made some apology for so worrying her, or thanked her for rescuing him, but he acted as if it had never happened.

Preparations for the visit to Brighton went on, and the summer days turned hot and humid, and everyone's tempers grew short. Melissa found herself counting the days till their departure, for she felt she could not bear to answer one more question from Nancy, who seemed to talk of nothing else, or listen one more time to Rob's flights of fancy about the many delights in store.

He treated his older sister with superiority, which infuriated her, tinged as it was with a faint air of disapproval which she could in no way explain. One afternoon after she had been out riding to check the condition of a newly reclaimed field, and was feeling hot and dirty and disheveled, she came across him on her return strolling around the gardens, immaculately dressed in town clothes. She felt immediately resentful. She had been doing *his* work, after all! That field was *his* responsibility, not hers! She might have kept her temper if he had not laughed at her appearance and said to her with a sneer, "Ah, how the mighty are fallen! Is this the latest Incomparable? What would your London beaux think if they could see you now, dear sister?"

Melissa exploded. In no uncertain terms she told him what she thought of him, going back to his falling into debt and causing everyone such great concern, as well as his behavior since he had returned from school.

"Lord of the Manor!" she said scornfully. "Too proud to see to his own inheritance! Why, 'tis a veritable Beau Brummell we have here, afraid to soil the tops of his boots! Do not concern yourself with me, brother! I do not care in the slightest what society thinks of me!"

Goaded into a reply, for the Beau was Rob's idol, he said quickly, "And that is a very good thing! After whistling two of the greatest catches of the season away, who do you think would consider you now?"

Melissa's eyes narrowed. "What are you talking about? What do you mean, *two* catches?"

Rob would have ended the argument right there for he was ashamed of his gambling debt and the fact he had not been more helpful since his return, but Melissa was determined to have the information she sought, and made him tell her.

One of his school friends had not hesitated to inform him after a trip to town, that his sister had made herself the *on-dit* of the year by declining to marry Lord Warner. As he blurted this out, Melissa said more calmly, "Yes, that is so. I could not marry a man who loved another. But you spoke of *two* catches, Rob! Come, tell me the whole!"

"I can only assume you have refused the Duke of Colchester as well," he said with asperity. "Why else would the man pay my gambling debt unless he hoped to become one of the family?"

Melissa started and grasped his arm. "The duke paid your debt? But . . . but, I went to Mr. Bentley and he said he would see to it!"

Rob shook his head over her naivete. "Obviously the duke got to him first. How foolish you were, Lissa, to let him escape! He is even richer than Lord Warner, and he must have wanted you very badly to pay *my* debt!"

Melissa turned away in confusion and Rob continued, for now the secret was out, he was anxious to talk about it. "I shall never forget the letter that accompanied the draft he sent me, never! If that was not the sign of a man in love . . ."

Melissa looked up eagerly. "What did he say, Rob?"

Her brother had the grace to redden as he replied, "I have it by heart although I burned it after the first reading! He said— 'Master Rob! If ever I find you are distressing your sister again, I will immediately post down to your school and give you the thrashing you so richly deserve! Yours, etc., Northrup.' Whew! It gives me the shivers just to remember it!" He looked carefully at his sister's bemused face and could not refrain from adding, "So you see, sister, you have lost him as well as Lord Warner! And you set yourself up as such a paragon, awake on every suit! I think you have behaved like a perfect ninny!"

Melissa bent her head and said softly, "Indeed, I fear you are right, Rob!"

She turned away without another word and went into the house, leaving her brother gaping after her.

The day of departure came and went, and Melissa, who had been very quiet since Rob's disclosure was glad when her brother and sister finally left. She had to think, and it was impossible to do so while the house was in such a turmoil of preparations. As the Throckmorton coach tooled away down the drive, she felt a pang of envy which she quickly stifled, and hurried away to saddle Captain and ride as hard as she could over the countryside. At last she came to Byway Brook on her way home, and slid from Captain's back to sit by the stream and ponder.

But he did not want to marry me, she told herself.

He never said such a thing, never, nor acted it either! He was only trying to win the wager! She remembered the first time she had seen the duke, right here at Byway Brook, and his insolent inspection of her face and figure, and had to smile a little to herself. Such a great rake, the duke! And then she remembered the three kisses he had given her, and her face grew warm. Were they the kisses of a man in love, or merely those of an accomplished lover, sure of his reception by an impressionable miss in her first season? She did not know. She stared into the water bubbling merrily over the stones and saw nothing but his face. That devil's grin, those sparkling black eyes!

She remembered how angry he had been when he found her in the garden with Lord Warner. Could it be possible that he *was* in love? Surely even the loss of all that money to the wager would not make a man so infuriated, would it?

How long she lingered by the brook she did not know, but when at last Captain whinnied to her and she realized it was growing late, she hastened to mount and ride home, no wiser than she had been before.

As she approached Wardley in the warm evening, she realized that a year had almost passed, and the wager was as good as won. Why hadn't the duke made a move in her direction? He must know where she was; he could get it out of Aunt Alice in a thrice! He does not want to marry me, and he has given up the wager, she thought sadly, wondering why she felt so despondent at this excellent reasoning. This was what she wanted, was it not? Now she would have the money she needed for Wardley Hall, without marrying a man she did not love.

As she gave Captain into Simon's care and walked up to the Hall, she wondered why she did not feel more triumphant at her success in besting the arrogant duke.

CHAPTER 13

Another Highwayman

It was just as well for Melissa's peace of mind that both the home farm and the kitchen garden produced heavy crops that summer. The hot, humid days had brought the fruit and vegetables to ripe profusion, and she did not have the time for any further introspection as she toiled long hours over the preserving kettle with cook and her aunt, or picked in the garden until she felt her back would break. Her London maid so kindly provided by Uncle Ferdie was astounded at her behavior, and when she was approached and asked to help, quickly turned in her notice and departed. Melissa watched her go with a small smile of regret. Jack could return from London now! There was no more danger that her elaborate hairdos and toilettes would tempt him. She was still careful to shade her complexion with a large bonnet, and wear gloves in the fields, but when she looked at her hands, purple with berry juice as she stirred the jam, she knew that Miss Melissa Ward, that Incomparable of Incomparables, was no more. It seemed to make her more cheerful, in spite of the hard work, and her Aunt Cardell breathed a sigh of relief. Whatever had been wrong with dear Lissa, Wardley had cured it at last!

One evening as the two sat in the drawing room after dinner, too tired even to talk, they heard the sound of urgent hooves on the drive. Melissa started up, exchanging a glance of alarm with her aunt. They heard Prims move slowly to answer the loud banging of the front door knocker, and to Melissa it seemed an age before the discreet knock at the drawing room door came, and he entered with a letter. Aunt Cardell took it with trembling hands, and Melissa moved behind her to read it over her shoulder.

She finished the short note long before her aunt did, and although she was stunned and frightened, was able to comfort her aunt when she moaned, "Dear Lord! Nancy sick and calling for you, Lissa! What are we to do? Oh, dear!"

Melissa stroked her hands and handed her her salts, and then she picked up the paper her aunt had let fall from nerveless fingers.

She frowned over the wording again. "Someone must have written this for Aunt Alice," she said thoughtfully. "It is not her hand. She does not mention the nature of Nancy's illness, how strange, and how like her! All it says is that Nancy wants me and I must make haste to join them in Brighton as soon as ever I can. Did you see the postscript, Aunt? We are not to worry, for the doctor is sure of her recovery!"

She turned to her aunt as she spoke these comforting words, for they had no time for hysterics now, only to find that redoubtable lady putting away her salts and straightening her cap with an air of determination. She had to smile through her fears, for Aunt Cardell always amazed her!

"We must go to Brighton in the morning!" the lady said firmly. "It is much too late to start tonight. Besides, we have no carriage and must hire one." She frowned. "Wherever are we to do that? It will delay us too much if we have to send Simon to Washburn but there is only the vicar's gig in the village!" She looked at her niece and added, "I know, my dear, but there is no way I can ride all the way to Brighton on horseback, even if you can! And I *must* go, Lissa! When your mother died at Nancy's birth, and I was sent for to take care of the family, why, it was like having the children I had never been fortunate to have before! And I raised Nancy from infancy; she is especially my own!" She sniffed and then brought her attention back to the problem at hand. "What are we to do?"

Melissa paced the floor, thinking furiously. Suddenly she whirled and exclaimed, "Aunt! Let me send Simon to the squire right now! I am sure he would lend us his carriage for such an errand as this, and Mrs. Holland is so fond of Nancy too! They will help us!"

Aunt Cardell agreed it was the perfect solution and set about writing a note to the Hollands while Melissa hurried to Simon's cottage. He was about to go to bed, but when he heard the bad news, he ran to the stable to saddle a horse. By the time he rode up to the front door, Melissa had the note in her hand. Telling him to be sure to give the answer to Prims when he returned, she went back to her aunt. Together they went to their rooms to pack a few necessities, for they had no idea how long they would be required to remain with Nancy. Melissa's mind was in a whirl as she threw gowns and slippers on the bed.

"Please, God," she prayed, "do not let anything happen to Nancy! Please do not let it be anything serious!" She put firmly from her mind all the horrible illnesses it might be in this hot summer weather, not at all reassured by the wording of the note, and was just finishing her packing when Prims brought the squire's answer. Of course they might have the carriage, and John Coachman too, and it would be at the gates of Wardley first thing in the morning. Aunt Cardell wept a little at his gruff kindness, and Mrs. Holland's few added sentences of concern, and then Melissa persuaded her to go to bed so as to be ready for an early start in the morning. She tried to follow her own advice, but it was a long time before she slept. Nancy ill! And she had been so impatient with her little sister before she left for Brighton!

They were on their way by half past eight the next morning. Melissa had hoped to start sooner, but Mrs. Cardell insisted on packing a large bandbox with every home remedy she could think of that might be required. Impatient to be off, Melissa asked John Coachman to make as much haste as possible, but he was an elderly man, long in the squire's service, and he had his own notions about the pace that should be maintained by members of the gentry. He insisted on stopping to rest the horses at Woking and at Horsham, and since neither Melissa or her aunt had the money for a change of teams, they were forced to comply. By late afternoon Melissa was ready to scream with vexation. They were still several miles from Brighton; it would be evening before they finally arrived! She and her aunt had tried to talk about other things during the long journey, but no matter what the topic, it was not long before they fell silent, each lost in her own thoughts and prayers.

Eventually they approached the outskirts of Brighton, and Melissa sat up straighter and smoothed her wrinkled gown. Suddenly, at the top of a small rise, a shot rang out. The coach crashed to a halt and both ladies were thrown from their seats. The coachman was swearing mightily above them as he tried to control the horses plunging in their traces when Melissa heard a powerful voice roar, "Stand and deliver!" She struggled back to her seat, knowing the elderly man on the box above them had no weapon, and had his hands full with the frightened team. Aunt Cardell was moaning with fear, and it was all Melissa could do to help her up from the untidy heap she had become on the floor of the coach. And all the while, a little voice in the back of her head was saying, "No! It cannot be! Even *he* would not go so far!"

The door of the coach was thrown open, and a tall, menacing figure peered inside. He was masked and caped, and wore a large hat pulled well down over his eyes. For a moment, Melissa felt a chill of real terror, but when the highwayman suddenly chuckled as he stared at them, any doubts she might have had swiftly disappeared. Instead, a cold wave of anger swept over her and she clenched her hands into fists.

"And wot 'ave we 'ere? Two gentry morts, I'll be bound!" he said in a coarse accent.

Aunt Cardell put out a trembling hand. "Oh, sir,

please let us go! We are riding to a young girl's sickbed and it is important that we reach Brighton as soon as possible! Here, we have but a little money, but please take it and let us go!"

She held up her reticule, offering it piteously to the highwayman. He seemed nonplussed by the gesture and bowed slightly.

"Keep your money, madam," he said in a completely changed voice. "That is not what I have come for!" And then, in an aside to another man still mounted and holding the highwayman's horse while he covered the coachman with a wicked looking pistol he ordered, "Watch him well, and when I have gone, release them and come to me!"

He strode even closer, and reached into the coach where Melissa was soothing her tearful aunt.

"Come, my dear," that soft, hated voice said, "it is you I have come for, as well you know!"

Aunt Cardell would have objected, but Melissa whispered, "Do not fear, Aunt! It is no ordinary highwayman at all, but the Duke of Colchester!"

While she was speaking, the highwayman reached into the coach and plucked her from her seat. She fought him as hard as she could, but he laughed at her efforts and threw her up before the saddle of his horse, nimbly following her before she could escape. He put one strong arm around her and holding her fast against him so she could hardly breathe, he turned again to the coach.

"Have no fear, Mrs. Cardell! Melissa will be restored to you unharmed as soon as we have concluded some unfinished business!"

He wheeled his horse and galloped off in the direction of Brighton. When they had left the coach safely behind them, he murmured in Melissa's ear,

"You really did not think I would let you win the wager in the end, did you, my dear? I meant what I said, you know; the Northrups never draw back, and it seemed such poetic justice to kidnap you in the disguise you yourself used!"

Melissa did not answer. She had never been so angry in her life; she felt if she spoke she would explode with fury, but helpless as she was, there was nothing to be done now. The duke rode easily through the streets of Brighton until he reached an impressive house on The Front. A man was waiting for them at the steps, Findle, Melissa saw with loathing, as the duke dismounted and lifted her down. When she would have run away, he swept her into his arms and climbed the steps to the front door. Melissa tried to beat him with her fists, but the duke just laughed at her efforts, and carried her through a small hall to a drawing room where he set her carefully on her feet. In an instant she was upon him, striking as hard as she could and crying, "You horrible creature! How could you do such an infamous thing?"

The duke captured her hands in one of his big ones and stood well out of the reach of her kicking feet.

"Steady on, wildcat!" he exclaimed. "How else was I to get you to come to Brighton after dear Lady Throckmorton ordered you from her door? Besides, the note said clearly that there was nothing to worry about, that Nancy would recover!"

"Oh, yes," Melissa panted, still struggling, "and that is just the sort of thing Aunt Alice would write, even if her niece was dying! She couldn't be bothered with a serious illness, so she would decide that all was well, no matter how sick Nancy was! When I think how fearful and worried Aunt Cardell and I have been, I could run you through!"

The duke looked at her in consternation. "I never thought of that, but of course I see you are right! You must accept my apologies!"

"Never, as long as I live, will I forgive you! You are as bad as Aunt Alice, thinking only of your own concerns, with no thought or compassion for others! Oh, how I hate you!"

The duke stared at her, his face now pale with distress. "Melissa, we must talk, and I find it impossible to do so while you are trying to strike me and kick me! Wherever did you learn such hoydenish manners? If you promise me to sit down quietly, I shall release you and not touch you again! Word of a Northrup!"

Melissa would have retorted, but she could see he would never allow her to hurt him, so she nodded her head curtly. She was instantly released and the duke walked away from her to remove his cloak and the large hat he wore. As Melissa sank down on a sofa breathlessly, she was indignant to see that beneath the enveloping cloak he was dressed in his usual elegant style, his boots gleaming with blacking, his coat snug to those powerful shoulders, his cravat without so much as an errant crease. It made her doubly furious, knowing as she did that she must look a complete romp in her wrinkled, dirty gown and road dusty face, with her curls every which way on her head. She stared at him with loathing, her chin high, and the duke had the grace to redden slightly. He took the seat across from her and leaned forward.

"Let me speak, Melissa, if you please, before you continue to villify me! I do most humbly apologize for your worries—I never considered the effect such a note would have on you or your aunt! Perhaps I am as bad as you say, but I never meant to alarm you; my one concern was to see you again." He paused, but she did not speak, so he continued. "When you left London so abruptly, and Lord Warner looked so morose and disappointed in the days thereafter, I guessed you had refused his offer. I knew you would never agree to marry him!" The duke rose and began to pace the drawing room. "He is not for such as you, my dear! I had the whole story from Ferdie, you know; he was so distressed at the way Lady Throckmorton sent you off, he could not keep it to himself! And for a woman with your hot blood, a marriage of convenience would never do!"

He smiled at her brilliantly, and Melissa said softly, "I am reconsidering my decision, Your Grace! Lord Warner has been kind enough to tell me he will wait for me. After today, I view his suit with a great deal more favor! Better a marriage of convenience than being at the mercies of such as you!"

The duke laughed ruefully. "Don't be such a little fool, Lissa! It would never do, and besides, you know you love me as much as I love you! We are two of a kind! The reason I held up your coach tonight was to tell you I wanted to marry you—let the wager go! I found out in London when I saw Lord Warner holding your hands how furious it made me that he should dare to touch you, and after you were gone, I missed you so sorely that I knew I had at last found my duchess! And if you are honest, you will admit that all I have to do is take you in my arms and kiss you . . ."

Melissa put up her hand and said sweetly, "But I have the word of a Northrup that you will do no such thing, do I not, Your Grace? If you touch me, I shall have to acknowledge that nothing, not even your word, is sacred to you!"

The duke who had been walking towards her, stopped abruptly, his face darkening in a ferocious frown. He spread out his hands helplessly. "You have me at *point non plus,* for you do have my word. Now why," he asked himself musingly, "was I so silly as to make such a rash promise? Very well, I shall tell you what is in my heart without touching you!"

Melissa rose from the sofa. "Do not put yourself to the trouble, Your Grace. You have *my* word, the word of a Ward, that I would not marry you for any reason, ever in my life!" She swept him a perfunctory curtsey. "And now, if you would be so kind, please call for a servant to take me to my uncle Throckmorton's house. Surely my aunt has been troubled long enough!"

The duke would have detained her, but one glance at her still angry face and snapping eyes told him it would be no use. He went to the drawing room door and opened it for her.

"I shall do myself the honor of escorting you to your uncle's house," he said formally. Minton hastened to hand him his hat and cane and to open the front door. He bowed low to Melissa as if she were a grand lady instead of the disheveled, furious miss that passed him.

The duke did not try to take her arm, but pointed the direction with his cane. " 'Tis only a few doors; Brighton is such a small place compared to London, we are all very cozily situated here."

Melissa did not reply to this pleasantry, nor did she speak when they reached the steps of the

Throckmortons' summer residence a few houses away. Johnson, the butler, answered her knock, and not being as well schooled as Minton could not help gaping at her as she swept inside and said, "The duke does not stay! Be so kind as to inform Lord and Lady Throckmorton that Miss Ward is arrived. And Johnson, has my aunt Mrs. Cardell come before me? I have been regrettably delayed!"

She heard the front door close softly behind her on the duke but she did not turn around. The butler told her that Mrs. Cardell was even then closeted with her uncle in the library, and asked her if she wished to retire for a moment before she joined them. Melissa glanced down at her wrinkled gown and saw that more than a few minutes would have to be spent for her to appear presentable, so she asked to be taken to the library immediately.

When he announced her, Lord Throckmorton jumped to his feet and rushed to hold her saying, "Dear Melissa! You are safe!"

She hugged him back and would have wept, but the voice of her aunt stayed her. "Lissa! It was the duke then, as you said? I have been telling my Lord Throckmorton the story and he finds it hard to believe!"

Her uncle led her to a seat and poured her a glass of wine. "Here, sit down and drink this, my dear! We have a thousand questions, but they can wait until you compose yourself."

As Melissa gratefully sipped the wine he added, "Mrs. Cardell has told me about the nefarious scheme that was planned to draw you here! Do not fear; Nancy is quite all right, you know! In fact she is enjoying her first visit to the theater with Rob and Alice." When he saw the tiny frown creasing Melissa's brow, he added quickly, "Do not worry about your reception by Lady Throckmorton, I beg you! You are welcome to stay with us as long as you like!"

Melissa smiled at him mistily. Her uncle had changed indeed if he were willing to face Aunt Alice's wrath!

She told her story simply, as if she had been through so much she did not have the strength to elaborate. Her uncle exclaimed at each new revelation, and interrupted with so many questions she thought the tale would never be told. Aunt Cardell merely stared at her, for this was the first time she had heard about the wager, and she watched her niece carefully.

Beginning with her adventures as a highwayman and her kidnapping by the duke and fortunate escape, to her joining the Throckmortons in London and further difficulties in fending off Tony Northrup, she spared herself nothing. Her uncle grew agitated, and several times murmured to himself, "Pon rep!" or "Is it possible?" and once "My good heavens!" When she reached the end he came to her and took her hands in his. "My dear child! But why did you not tell me? I could have helped you, you know, even if Alice . . ." he stumbled and did not finish while Melissa squeezed his hands gratefully.

"I thought I could handle it myself, Uncle Ferdie. After all, it was through my machinations that I became involved with him! But it is all over now! In a few days the year of the wager will be over and I shall be free of the duke forever!" She seemed more sad and regretful than angry and relieved, and Aunt Cardell made a movement as if she wished to speak. When the other two looked to her, she shook her head, and sat back in her chair.

"But you must not tell Aunt Alice, Uncle!" Melissa exclaimed, holding tight to both his hands. "Make up some story, please! I cannot bear for her to know about the duke, or . . . or anything else!"

Lord Throckmorton frowned a little. "But what can we tell her, Melissa? You know she will never understand why you and Mrs. Cardell have arrived unless she knows the truth. Do not be harsh with her, my dear! I know she has not always treated you kindly, but you are family after all, and when I have explained it . . ."

Melissa begged him again not to speak, and Mrs. Cardell took a hand. "Lord Throckmorton," she said, "I think it best for Melissa to go to bed now! She has been through a great deal today and we can discuss this again in the morning when she is not so tired."

When he would have spoken, she gave him a warning glance, and helped Melissa up. Lord Throckmorton summoned the housekeeper and Melissa was soon following her up the stairs to the guest bedroom she would share with Mrs. Cardell.

When the door at last closed behind her, Lord Throckmorton threw out his hands and said, "It is all very well, Mrs. Cardell, but what are we to tell Lady Throckmorton?"

"I propose that we tell her the truth, no matter what Melissa wants!" Mrs. Cardell said tartly. "I think when we explain to the lady that her niece is about to become the Duchess of Colchester, it will remove any objections she might have about entertaining her again!" Privately she thought that even Lady Throckmorton must want to stand in well with a duchess, but she did not voice that sentiment!

Ferdie hemmed and hawed. "Well, yes, of course you are right I suppose. The duke will have to marry

her now he has compromised her name. I can insist
on that! But . . . but, do you think dear Melissa will
ever agree? She was so vehement against him!"

Mrs. Cardell laughed softly. "Oh, yes, I heard her,
but I know my niece!"

"Pon my word, Mrs. Cardell," Lord Throckmorton
broke in, "are you sure? She hates him! Heard . . .
heard her say so m'self!"

Mrs. Cardell rose and gathered her pelisse and
reticule. "You may safely trust me in this matter,
m'lord. And now, I am really very tired! Perhaps it
would be wise to say nothing of our arrival until
tomorrow? I will be up betimes to speak to Lady
Throckmorton. May I suggest that you do not mention any of this until I have had a chance to explain
to her?"

Lord Throckmorton was not hard to convince that
this would be the best course, and before long both
travelers were fast asleep, long before Lady Throckmorton and her two charges came home from the
theater. Lord Throckmorton warned the butler sternly
to remain mum about the evening, and cravenly left
the house so he would not be tempted to betray any
secret when Alice returned.

CHAPTER 14

The End of the Wager

The next morning, Lady Throckmorton had an unwelcome visitor with her morning chocolate. Ferdie waited nervously in the drawing room that overlooked the street, wishing now he had told Mrs. Cardell how dear Alice hated to be approached before she was dressed! Rob had already gone out, and Nancy, worn out with excitement, was still asleep as was her big sister when Mrs. Cardell knocked on Lady Throckmorton's door and shut it firmly behind her. The ladies were closeted for some time. At first, Lady Throckmorton had been inclined to be indignant at the intrusion, but it was not long before a gurgle of amusement and amazement escaped her.

"You cannot mean, dear Mrs. Cardell—What a sly puss!—Why, not the *duke!*—It never crossed my mind!—A highwayman?—Kidnapped?—Well, *I* never suspected! And to think I knew nothing about it!"

Before she could become upset at being left out of

the plot, Mrs. Cardell continued. "Lady Throckmorton! It is imperative we keep Melissa here for a few days. I do not think the duke will let it rest; he is bound to try and see her again, and I am sure she is in love with him!" She paused and then asked seriously, "I have never met the duke, Lady Throckmorton. Is he . . . is he a *good* man? I know he is a favorite with our neighbor Squire Holland, but I have heard he is a rake!"

Lady Throckmorton did not dismiss Mrs. Cardell's worries carelessly. "I can assure you, Mrs. Cardell, that Tony Northrup is no where near as bad as he has been painted! He is no innocent boy, of course, but Melissa is no simpering young miss herself! They will be perfect for each other!"

Reassured, Mrs. Cardell continued. "But what can we do to promote the match? And how can you pretend to welcome Melissa after you dismissed her so abruptly in London?"

Lady Throckmorton had the grace to blush, but she tossed her head and said firmly, "It is quite simple! I have changed my mind, that is all! I often do! I shall apologize very prettily to Melissa for being so cross with her in London and beg her pardon! I am sure I can convince her that I want her to stay for some time and visit us. And yes," she added, setting down her chocolate cup decisively, "you can say that you told me that you were on your way to visit friends, but an accident to your coach forced you to seek shelter here last night. She will know that for the crammer it is, but it saves face without her having to tell me the whole! Please to hand me that dressing gown, Mrs. Cardell! We have a great deal to do, and I must get up!"

Aunt Cardell did as she was bid, realizing that she

was now relegated to the background while Lady Throckmorton took charge of the approaching nuptials. Still she hesitated.

"My lady, we must be very careful not to let Melissa know that we suspect she is in love with the duke! That would be fatal!"

"Pooh, I know that!" Lady Throckmorton said, tossing her head and ringing for her maid. "I will not so much as refer to him; in fact I may not mention Lord Warner either. I shall be very busy presenting a most charming young man I have met here, all the while whispering to Melissa that he is worth three thousand a year! She will suspect nothing!"

Mrs. Cardell had to admit that Lady Throckmorton seemed to know what she was about, and went down to reassure that lady's husband that all was well, and Lady Alice was firmly on their side. He sighed in relief!

As they walked to the hall, the knocker sounded and the butler accepted two large bouquets. One he presented to Mrs. Cardell who smiled as she read the inscription. The other was dispatched to Melissa's room. Mrs. Cardell showed the note to Lord Throckmorton; a most humble and abject apology from the duke for so disturbing her. He asked permission to call and tender his regrets in person, but this Mrs. Cardell was not permitted to allow. When Lady Throckmorton heard of it, she firmly declared the duke was *persona non grata* for the moment. "For Mrs. Cardell, if we allow him to run tame here, it will drive Melissa away immediately! Let me speak to him!"

Melissa refused her flowers with loathing, and sent them back with no acknowledgment, the card unopened, and the duke spent a miserable morning until he met Lady Throckmorton walking in the Pavilion gardens. She strolled up and down with him for some time, whispering some very interesting words in his ear, and he went home much more lighthearted and encouraged!

Melissa was surprised that her Aunt Alice was so polite and gracious. She could only believe that her uncle had finally asserted himself for the lady to beg her pardon so nicely, and she was relieved that Aunt Alice did not know the true story. She agreed to stay on for a few days to see Rob and Nancy, and allow Mrs. Cardell a chance to enjoy the seaside.

She kept the date of the wager's termination firmly in her mind. It was only five days away, and she fully intended to stay until then. She considered for a long time the best way of handling the situation when the duke should come to pay his debt, and many long moments were spent daydreaming on which would be the most humiliating and humbling to him! She was at first inclined to refuse to see him at all, only sending him a stiff, formal note asking him to remit the money to Mr. Bentley since she had no desire to ever set eyes on him again, but she quickly discarded that since it would give her no opportunity to observe his defeat firsthand. Besides, she would have to ask him to subtract the money he had advanced to Rob to pay his gambling debts, and thank him, and that would make the note extremely complicated and difficult to write. Perhaps she should just receive him coldly, not ask him to sit down, and then just accept the money without a word. How she wished she had the courage to throw it in his hateful face! It bothered her very much that she needed the money so badly for Wardley, for surely that would be the most supremely satisfying gesture of all!

Melissa refused to attend any evening parties, to Aunt Alice's distress. She had brought nothing suitable to wear, and even though she was now as elegantly coiffed as she had been in London, she would not appear to advantage in the simple morning gowns she had packed as suitable to attend a sickroom. She consented to stroll along The Front with Nancy in the mornings to enjoy the fresh salt air, and agreed to try the bathing machines drawn up on the strand with her, but even Aunt Alice's hints about the handsome and wealthy Mr. Wickwood could not tempt her from her seclusion. She had no desire to see the duke before the day she was so impatiently awaiting.

Mrs. Cardell tried to get her to reminisce about their adventure, but she refused curtly. "Let us never think of it again, Aunt! Horrible, arrogant creature! So sure of his omnipotence. Ha!"

From which statement Mrs. Cardell gathered that the duke might have a harder row to hoe than she had imagined. She assured Melissa that she had quite forgiven the young man, and her niece said coldly, "That is very Christian of you, Aunt, but *I* shall never forgive him!"

On the day that Melissa had held up the duke's coach the year before, she was up early, and was not surprised to receive a formal note from him begging the indulgence of a few moments of her time to complete a transaction he was sure she remembered. She sent a curt reply, indicating that three o'clock would be the most agreeable to her. Now why did I say three, she wondered? To make him wait as long as possible and thus ruin his day? She decided it must be that, and not the fact that that was the most private time, for Rob and Nancy were going riding, and she had heard Aunt Alice inviting Mrs. Cardell to join them in their carriage for an afternoon ride through the countryside.

At two, Melissa summoned her aunt's dresser and had her redo her hair. She donned her prettiest gown, which she had had freshened the day before. By two-thirty she was in the drawing room leafing through a copy of *Belle Assemblée*. It must have been a very dull issue, for even the plate of the most ravishing new gown from France was quickly flipped over.

Promptly at three, Johnson knocked and asked if she would receive the Duke of Colchester. She stood up, her heart beating fast as he entered the room, his face pale above his faultless morning dress. After Johnson had bowed himself out and closed the door, she remembered that she should have asked him to bring the duke some wine, but her head was in such a whirl, she had completely forgotten such social amenities. The duke bowed to her formally, and she asked him to be seated in a small, cold voice. He advanced until he was standing close before her and said stiffly, "My compliments, Miss Ward! You are the victor after all—a most formidable opponent! The sum we agreed on is in this envelope."

He watched her carefully as she took it, upset by his nearness, and then she knew she could not accept money won in such a way, not for Wardley, not for anything!

She held it out to him and said, "I will not accept the money, Your Grace! I should have never made the wager to begin with, and it has brought me nothing but grief! Besides, you paid Rob's debt unbeknownst to me. It was kind of you, and . . . and I thank you, but I cannot accept the money!"

The duke seemed surprised. "Not accept it? But it was fairly won, was it not?"

"Of course," Melissa admitted, her lips wooden. She wondered if he noticed how strange her voice sounded, or how dry her lips were? He did not take the envelope from her hand, but moved away to stand by the fireplace.

"Perhaps you feel you have *not* won it, Miss Ward?" he asked idly. Melissa stared at him.

"Whatever can you mean, *not* won it?" she asked.

He came towards her again. "I mean, my dear, that you know you are in love with me after all, even if you will not be honest enough to admit it, so therefore you have not won the wager!"

Melissa stiffened and hit him as hard as she could, and then took a quick step backwards for the duke looked so dangerous with his cheek red from her blow that she was really frightened by what she saw in his eyes.

Quickly he came to her and grasped her by the arms, shaking her so hard she thought her head would fall off her neck, and saying through clenched teeth, "Never do that again, do you hear me? Never! I have behaved very badly, it is true, but you are no innocent yourself, my dear highwayman! You are guilty of just as serious misconduct, so do not play the injured young lady with me!" His tone softened, and he looked down into her eyes, now brimming with tears.

"Ah, Lissa," he groaned, "how can I be angry with you when I love you so much? You are frustrating, maddening, exciting, and a darling, and I must have you or I shall never be happy! Tell me truly, if you can, that you do not love me!"

He stared down into her face, and when she did

not speak, he said, "I knew you could not lie about it! You *do* love me, don't you?"

He gave her a little shake, and she said weakly, "Odious man! Yes, for my sins, I admit I do!"

The duke laughed out loud as he pulled her close to him, and then he bent his head and kissed her possessively. For the first time, Melissa let herself drown in that kiss and return it freely.

It was some time later as they were sitting together on the sofa with Tony's arms firmly around his love, that she glanced down and saw the money all over the carpet.

"Oh, Tony, look! We must pick that up before Aunt Alice arrives and sees it! You must take it away with you, promise me! I should never have agreed to such an infamous wager! I wonder you can love someone so brazen!"

The duke grinned at her lazily. "Very easily, my love!" he said, with such a note in his voice that she blushed and hid her face in his coat.

"And if you will not accept the money, you will just have to spend it as the Duchess of Colchester! But stay! Perhaps we should use it for your bride journey to be sure it does not return to haunt us! Where would you like to go, my love?"

Melissa said she had no idea and would leave it up to him and the duke mused, "Perhaps Italy? No, that would never do for the roads are infested with *banditi!* And Greece is worse! Now where in the world can we go and escape highwaymen?"

Melissa hit him with a sofa pillow. "Am I never to be allowed to forget my illegal adventures? I assure you, m'lord, I intend to be a very paragon of virtue from now on!"

The duke kissed her again and murmured, "Dearest

Lissa, please do not! I prefer my hoyden! And to make sure you are ever reminded of my wishes . . ."

He set her from him firmly, and went to the door and called the very interested butler to bring the things he had brought with him. Johnson's eyes popped as he entered with a large bouquet and a small box, and he was set to picking up the most money he had ever seen from the drawing room carpet. When he had collected it and handed it back to the duke, he was sent for some of Lord Throckmorton's best champagne. It was a test few butlers could have handled so dispassionately.

Melissa admired the flowers and watched the duke in wonder as he opened the box to disclose a beautiful diamond. "The betrothal ring of the Northrups, my dear!" he said, putting it on her finger. "It is yours until our oldest son requires it for his bride!"

Melissa blushed and exclaimed over it, but Tony was not done. "*That* is not what will remind you of my wishes, love! Here is your wedding ring!" He held out a wide gold band, and Melissa looked at him inquiringly.

"You do not recognize it? I had it made from Mr. Colbert's gold watch that you took from him on your first try at the high toby! That should remind you that I prefer my highwayman to any starched-up and proper duchess!"

Melissa had to laugh and then she ran to him, tears of happiness in her eyes.

When he would have kissed her again, she put the hand with the large diamond on it across his lips. He looked at her, one black brow raised, and she said, "Very well, Your Grace, but be warned that I intend to be a very good duchess for all of that!"

The duke held her tightly and murmured, "I shall see to that, scamp!"

What Johnson, that staid and proper butler, thought of the goings-on in the front drawing room that afternoon, he never said, but when the Throckmortons and Mrs. Cardell arrived home, he announced pompously, "You will wish to join Miss Ward and the Duke of Colchester, m'lord, m'lady, Mrs. Cardell. They have been in the drawing room for over an hour!"

Mrs. Cardell and the Throckmortons embraced each other happily, exclaiming and smiling, and when the excitement died down Johnson asked woodenly,

"Will *more* champagne be required, m'lord?"

ABOUT THE AUTHOR

Barbara Ward Hazard was born and raised in Fall River, Massachusetts. After receiving a B.F.A. in advertising design from the Rhode Island School of Design, she worked as a technical editor, an advertising artist and an advertising freelancer.

In 1968, Barbara Hazard began studying oil painting with Amy Jones and since then has sold 25 major works and had two one-man and numerous group shows in North Westchester and Vermont.

Writing, she says, is the most satisfying and the easiest of anything she has ever attempted. She looks forward to many more years at the typewriter.

She is married and has three sons, Steven, David and Scott.

Let COVENTRY Give You
A Little Old-Fashioned Romance